OPERATOR #5

Purple armies from the prairies and a great Purple navy looming over the western horizon made ready to clamp the fetters of slavery on America's last defenders. But a grim line of fighting men waited in the Emperor Rudolph's path with a soldierly serenity that said, "Here we die." And every life laid on this altar of freedom gave Jimmy Christopher, Operator 5 of the Intelligence, new respite as he followed a trail of desperate adventure studded with disgrace and death.

Liberty's Suicide Legions

THE OPERATOR #5 SERIES

Liberty's Suicide Legions

BY CURTIS STEELE

Cover painting by John Hewitt
Interior illustrations by J. Fleming Gould

WILDSIDE PRESS

In the far reaches of High Asia, the Purple Empire had set up its factories and its smelters, to forge the most powerful weapon yet devised in military history. That weapon was a fleet of super-dread-noughts equipped with a strange secret device to render our Defense Force helpless. . . . In this gripping novel of the historic Purple Invasion, giant guns ashore, and turret magic at sea hurl death at America's crumbling bulwarks as intrigue knifes the stout defenders. And Operator 5, Secret Service ace, becomes a man without a country, with death and disgrace as his only reward.

CHAPTER ONE

Plan Z

THE BLOOD-RED SUN, rising out of the East, threw glinting

streaks of light athwart the conning towers of a hundred massive ships steaming across the Pacific.

Long, graceful, deadly eighteen-inch guns, the largest ever mounted on a battleship, yawned with open muzzles, ready to hurl their charges of thunder and destruction at the coast of California, toward which the great fleet was heading. Tampions had been removed from the guns, and the decks cleared for action.

From the halyards of each of those ships rippled the crimson flag of the Central Empire, bearing the gruesome insignia of the severed head and the crossed broadswords. It was under this flag that the Purple Emperor, the master of the Central Empire, had conquered Europe and Asia, and was even now pressing home his conquest of the United States. Two hundred and forty days ago, the mighty forces of the Purple Empire had landed on the eastern seaboard of America, and had marched irresistibly westward until now they were encamped under the shadows of the Rocky Mountains. And in the meantime this mighty fleet was sailing from Asia to clamp down the second jaw of the trap; the American Defense Force was to be caught between two fires — the booming artillery of the Purple Army from the east; and the mighty guns of the fleet from the west.

Behind the fleet were the smoking ruins of Hawaii and the other American islands in the Pacific, reduced to smoldering wreckage by the terrific bombardment of these floating forts. Now, the California coast would soon be within range.

Aboard the *C.E.S. Koenig,* flagship of this tremendous naval force, Admiral Baroda, supreme commander of the Eastern Fleet of the Central Empire, sat in conference with a dozen squadron commanders. Baroda's brilliant scarlet uniform, bedecked with decorations representing orders of the Central Empire, made a good match for his ruddy, red-veined face. Thick hands rested on the chart before him upon the long conference table, and the squadron commanders listened to him attentively.

"Gentlemen," he was saying in the thick, guttural language of the Central Empire, "we have struck the first blow at the American defenses in the Pacific. There is now not a single American fortification between California and Yokohama. Nothing stands between us and the American coast. Within ten hours, according to radio instructions from His Imperial Majesty, Rudolph I, we arrive within sight of San Francisco, and begin the bombardment!"

His wide under-lip curled with arrogance as he went on. "Nothing can withstand our huge guns. Our twelve airplane carriers will release five hundred bombers to fly up and down the coast spreading destruction while we demolish San Francisco. The operation promises to be entirely successful. Within five hours after starting the bombardment we should be able to land our marines to march eastward to effect a junction with the land troops at the Rocky Mountains. Gentlemen, let us drink to the new conquest!"

The officers at the table raised the champagne glasses which had been set before them by stewards, and drank the toast offered by their admiral. Baroda drained his glass, then held it up between his thick fingers, slowly exerted pressure. The fragile stem of the glass snapped. "So," he said, "will we snap the backbone of the American resistance — for the glory of Rudolph I, Emperor of the World!"

All around the table champagne glasses snapped as the squadron commanders broke into excited talk.

A PETTY OFFICER ENTERED, saluted smartly, and laid a wireless message on the table before the admiral. "This was received over the radio, Your Lordship."

Baroda read it, flushed with pride, and arose. The squadron commanders fell silent and the admiral said: "I will read aloud this radio message from Baron Flexner. 'Congratulations on your wonderful victory in the Pacific Islands. His Imperial Majesty is proud of you and of the fleet. Radio us as soon as you arrive within range of San Francisco, and His Majesty will himself give the word to begin firing. Our troops will simultaneously launch offensive against Americans entrenched in the Rocky Mountains. Execute immediately all American prisoners captured at Hawaii and Guam. Be prepared to employ Plan Z if American planes offer resistance to your progress. Again, congratulations!'

"The radio message was signed by Baron Julian Flexner, the Prime Minister of His Imperial Majesty, Rudolph I."

Baroda laughed unpleasantly. "Execute all prisoners!" he repeated. "I have been awaiting permission to hang them all. We will do so before lunch."

He glanced around the table, saw the puzzled glances of his officers. He chuckled. "I see that you are all curious about the reference in this message to Plan Z, is it not?"

There were several eager nods and expressions of curiosity from the squadron commanders. "Well, as you know, Plan Z has been veiled in secrecy. You all have wondered about the peculiar auxiliary turrets on our capital ships. You know that each of those turrets has been closed to all ships' officers, even to the captains and executive officers, and that they have been in charge of squads of picked men who do not leave even to eat."

"That is true, Your Lordship," one of the squadron commanders said. "We have thought that perhaps the turrets concealed some new engine of war —"

"Exactly! We are informed that the Americans have a large force of airplanes in San Francisco Bay, which they bought from a South American manufacturer."

"Yes, Your Lordship. We have heard that the American planes are of a new design, originated by that devil who is known as Operator 5, and that they are probably swifter than our own bombers. If they should attack —"

Baroda chuckled again, wickedly. "If they should attack, Captain Wilhelm, you will then see those turrets in operation. I promise you that not a single American plane will return to its base!"

There was a startled silence among the Central Empire Naval officers, that lasted for almost a minute. Then they burst into a rousing cheer, as they understood the import of the admiral's words.

Baroda rubbed his hands. "And now, the prisoners. Each of our ships has its quota. Instruct the units under your command to erect gibbets on the decks. The executions will take place promptly at noon!"

He arose, and all the officers snapped promptly to their feet, stood at attention, then followed him out to the bridge. Here, Baroda proudly gazed across the ocean.

As far as the eye could reach in every direction, the sleek struc-

ADMIRAL BARODA

tures of the mighty ships of the line under his command steamed squadron by squadron, with battle pennants flying. Flanking the great ships were countless destroyers and light cruisers, while far to the rear the supply ships followed.

The *Koenig* sailed in advance of the mighty armada, except for a contingent of destroyers and a cruiser which acted as scouts. Overhead dozens of planes circled above the fleet, taking off from the twelve mother-ships.

Baroda's chest expanded, and his small eyes gleamed with pride. "Such a fleet," he said more to himself than to the others, "has never been assembled before in the history of the world. There is nothing — *nothing* — that can stand against us!"

CHAPTER TWO

Fuel for War Fires

ABOUT THIRTY MILES ABOVE EL CENTRO, on the broad highway that skirts the fringe of the Imperial Valley in Southern California, a single automobile might have been seen driving northward at a steady pace of forty miles an hour. An aviator, looking down upon the scene from above, would have noted nothing peculiar about that car, except perhaps the small American flag fluttering from the radiator cap.

However, had there been an aviator at that spot at that time, and had he looked behind that car toward the Mexican border, he would at first have been startled and mystified. For in the gathering darkness, it would have seemed to him that all that highway stretching back toward El Centro was apparently moving northward like a quickly wriggling worm.

That sense of the movement of the road was, of course, an optical illusion fostered by the gathering darkness. The thing that was moving on the road was, in reality, a long line of huge gasoline tank trucks. These trucks, each with a capacity of 500 gallons, were moving northward on the highway behind the automobile, driving two abreast with an even space of 75 feet behind each truck. There were five hundred of these rolling tanks, and they stretched back for almost six miles along the highway.

At intervals of a half mile along this far-flung line there was a light tank — twelve of them in all — which acted as escort. This huge supply of gasoline was vital to the American defense against the invading troops of the Central Empire. Five hundred miles to the north, in San Francisco Bay, a huge fleet of American planes lay idle and useless for lack of fuel. American oil fields in the south and in the southwest had been either captured or destroyed by the steadily advancing machine of the Purple army. This supply of gasoline had been bought in Mexico, and was being rushed northward so that the American planes could once more go into action.

In the car at the head of the line rode the man who had negotiated the deal — Jimmy Christopher, known to the enemy as Operator 5. He drove silently now, staring ahead into the gathering night, while a thin sharp-featured little man with lively eyes in the seat beside him manipulated a short-wave radio receiving set.

This little man had proved of invaluable assistance to Operator 5 many times in the past. In the old days before the Purple invasion, Slips McGuire had been a member of the light-fingered gentry who made a living from the pockets of unsuspecting passengers in the subway systems of New York City.

Operator 5 had found him, had recognized the innate qualities of the man, and had understood that Slips McGuire's occupation at that time was more the result of environment than of a criminal bent. He had taken McGuire out of that sordid life, and though the little man was frequently tempted to use those long, nimble fingers of his, he had on the whole proved that Operator 5's estimate of his underlying character had been a good one. For he had become a valuable and loved member of Jimmy Christopher's small band of friends.

Now, while Jimmy Christopher drove steadily northward along the highway, with the Santa Rosa mountains on the left and the Salton Sea on the right, Slips McGuire was trying to get the short-wave broadcast from American headquarters in San Francisco. Suddenly a voice broke into the darkness out of the radio loudspeaker; calling *"O-5! O-5!"*

Slips McGuire exclaimed: "Jimmy! That's Z-7's voice. He's calling you!"

OPERATOR 5 NODDED, AND KEPT ON DRIVING at the same even pace of forty miles per hour. The voice that was coming over the radio was that of Z-7, the chief of the United States Intelligence Service — Operator 5's immediate superior, and the man who had taken charge temporarily of the American Defense forces at the time of the death of the President of the United States. The voice of Z-7 now came over the radio crisply, urgently; and the message he was delivering was of such startling importance that Jimmy Christopher's knuckles grew white as his hands tautened on the wheel.

"Operator 5!" Z-7 was saying. *"I am delivering this message at five-minute intervals in the hope that you will do something. Central Empire troops have broken through American defense line along the Colorado River. They are marching across the Imperial*

Valley now. If they intercept your gasoline trucks on El Centro Highway, all is lost. Gasoline essential. You must bring it through at all costs. Hesitate at no sacrifice. Signing off now. Will call again in five minutes."

As the radio grew silent, Slips McGuire glanced, wide-eyed, at Operator 5. "Jimmy! they are sure to spot us. If they turn a couple of guns on those gasoline tanks —"

Jimmy Christopher was glancing up at the sky out of the side window of the car. "There's one consolation anyway," he said grimly. "They won't be able to send up any planes tonight. With that low ceiling, a plane wouldn't have a chance to take off. At least, they can't bomb us from the air —"

Once more the radio came to life, and Z-7's voice, more urgent than ever, cut into the night: "O-5! O-5! I am hoping you will catch this message. Enemy troops have passed Calipatria, in Imperial Valley. Retreating Americans report that enemy is marching post-haste across country south of the Salton Sea, apparently to intercept highway at Kane Springs. This can only mean that they had advance information of the movement of gasoline trucks. Some traitor either with your column or here at headquarters has given them accurate news of your whereabouts. Not knowing your exact location I can give you no advice, but for God's sake, Jimmy, *save that gasoline!*"

Almost on the heels of Z-7's voice, there came the sound of shattering gunfire from the rear of the column.

Slips McGuire exclaimed hoarsely "Gawd, Jimmy, they've caught us!"

Tight-lipped, OPERATOR 5 BROUGHT THE CAR to a halt, and switched off the headlights. He sprang out of the car with Slips McGuire following him, and ran back toward the two leading trucks, which had stopped when he did. Each of those trucks carried a detail of four Americans, three of whom were armed with rifles or sub-machine guns, while the fourth did the driving. Now, as the long line rumbled to a halt, with the sound of intensive firing growing louder and quicker far to the rear, these Americans sprang down from the cabs of the trucks, and gathered hastily around Operator 5.

Jimmy Christopher shouted crisply: "Three men from each truck will form at the side of the road. The trucks will go on with one man apiece. Stop for nothing, and drive hell-bent for leather all through the night. Send word back to the tanks to pull out of line and form a rear guard. We are going to hold the enemy on the road while the trucks drive away. Get going now!"

He waved to the drivers of the foremost trucks, shouted: "Drive ahead."

The group of Americans about him and Slips was growing by the minute now, and far down the line they could see the shadowy bulk of the small American tanks pulling over to the side of the road to allow the trucks to pass.

One of the Americans, an older man, with hair greying at the temples, strode up beside Jimmy and said: "Better get in your car and lead the trucks, Operator 5. We'll take care of holding the enemy back."

Jimmy Christopher shook his head. "I'm staying with you, Cahill. Where did you get the idea that I'd leave you and the boys here to face the music without me?"

The Americans had already formed in column of twos at the side of the road and were running back toward the scene of the fighting at the rear.

Cahill glanced helplessly at Slips McGuire, then frowned at Jimmy Christopher. "Look here, Operator 5, I was a colonel in the National Guard, and I'm capable of taking charge of that rear-guard action. Maybe you don't know it, but those boys who are going back there now to stop the enemy are never going to leave this place alive. We're going to fight there until the last man of us is killed so as to give the trucks a good chance to get away. You're too damned valuable to be killed right now. You get in that car and drive ahead with McGuire. I'll take charge of everything here."

THE TRUCKS WERE RUSHING PAST THEM NOW, on their way again, at greatly accelerated speed. They flashed by swiftly, still two abreast, and the drivers waved as they passed the spot where Operator 5 stood. The word had gone down the line, and the guards from each truck had dismounted, were forming into companies and moving out into the fields on either side of the road.

Each half-company had an officer, and was acting in accordance with instructions previously issued by Jimmy Christopher for just such an emergency.

They were deploying on either side of the road, taking positions that would permit them to enfilade the enemy. Some fifty of the Americans, including Cahill, were gathered around Operator 5. This was also in accordance with instructions. These fifty would hold the center of the road, defending it against any of the Purple troops that passed the tanks.

Far behind, they could hear the shooting. Eight-inch naval guns those were, mounted on the new, huge tanks of the Central Empire — tanks capable of making a speed of sixty miles per hour. Those leviathans would ride down the American baby tanks, would be able to crush the resistance and catch up with the unwieldy column of trucks. Already, shells were screaming in the rear.

A half-dozen gasoline trucks had been cut off far back, apparently, and now a huge sheet of flame rose to the sky as a shell found its mark in the tank of one of those trucks. Bright. vermillion fire made the night bright.

Cahill exclaimed: "That's one of the last trucks in the column. It's down near Kane Springs. Look — my God, there must be twenty of the enemy tanks!"

The last of the gasoline trucks whizzed past, and now two big army trucks which had been riding close to the rear of the column pulled up alongside the group. These trucks were loaded with barbed wire, grenades, and two small trench mortars.

Operator 5 started to supervise the setting of the mortars, which could be fired from the specially constructed back platforms of the trucks. He set others to unloading the barbed wire, which he ordered erected on posts sunk into the ground on either side of the road. He instructed a dozen men to provide themselves with grenades.

"We'll have to stop those tanks right here, boys. Don't fire the mortars till they're within range. And save the grenades for the last —"

Cahill had taken Slips McGuire and three or four of the Americans aside, and was whispering to them. Now, he approached

Jimmy Christopher, followed by those others, and said firmly: "I'm sorry, Operator 5, but we're going to handle this business ourselves. You're needed in San Francisco. We can't risk losing you in an engagement of this kind. Maybe this is mutiny, but if it is, you can make the most of it. You get in that car with McGuire and drive away after the gasoline trucks, or we're going to send you away!"

Jimmy Christopher flushed deep red. "Damn it, Cahill, you'll obey orders. I'm in command of this column, and if I chose to remain here, you'll like it!"

Cahill looked to the others for encouragement, and they all nodded to him. He insisted doggedly: "There isn't much time for argument, Operator 5. There's the first of the enemy tanks, less than a mile away. They'll be firing down the road here any minute now. Are you going?"

"No!" Jimmy Christopher exploded. "By God, Cahill, I'll not be mollycoddled —"

Cahill nodded a signal to the others, and they suddenly closed in on Jimmy from all sides. He stared at them a moment in surprise, then, as he divined their purpose, he stepped back quickly and lashed out with both fists. He sent two of the men staggering, but they did not strike back, merely advanced on him.

Cahill said calmly: "It'll do you no good, Operator 5. Whether you like it or not, you're going to be kept out of danger."

JIMMY CHRISTOPHER'S LIPS WERE GRIM. He shouted to the men at the two supply trucks: "Come here, you fellows —"

His shout was broken off as the whole small group of them piled into him, dragging him down to the ground. He struggled, squirmed, striking at them mercilessly. But they clung to him grimly, and Slips McGuire, avoiding his eyes, tied his wrists behind him while they held him helpless. Then Slips tied his feet, and they lifted Operator 5 bodily, carried him into the car which had headed the column.

Jimmy's eyes were bleak. He said tightly as they sat him in the seat next the driver's: "Cahill, you've gone too far. I'll remember this —"

Cahill smiled. "Remember me, Operator 5. Remember all of us.

The chances are, none of us will survive this. Try to think well of us. We're doing what we think is best for the country!"

He waved his hand; and Slips McGuire, who had slid in under the wheel, put the car in gear and spurted forward. They left Cahill and his small group in the middle of the road. Those men were remaining behind to die, so that American planes could have gasoline. Cahill raised his hand in silent salute, then turned and led the others back to the supply trucks.

A shell from one of the approaching enemy tanks whined in the air, struck the road exactly between the two trucks. There was a thunderous, screeching detonation and a haze of smoke spread over the road.

As the smoke dissipated, a huge crater appeared in the road where the shell had struck. Bits of rock and concrete and human flesh flew through the air. Of Cahill and his companions there was no sign. Had Operator 5 remained there, he too would have been killed.

Now, all along the stretch of highway, rifles and machine guns, bursting grenades and the deep-toned detonations of the big enemy guns made a hell of the night. Fifteen hundred Americans were laying down their lives to stop the advance of a whole enemy division — so that the gasoline trucks could get through.

And in the car which Slips McGuire was driving, Operator 5 had twisted around in his seat, was looking back through the rear window at the road behind, which was brilliantly lighted by the flashes of the battle.

His lips were a tight, hard line as he swung on Slips McGuire. He said ominously: "Slips, untie my hands."

McGuire pretended not to hear, kept facing ahead, where he could see the last of the long column of trucks.

"Untie my hands, Slips," Jimmy repeated.

Slips didn't look at him, but shook his head quickly. "Nix, Jimmy. I'm not lettin' you go back there. I don't care what you do to me, but I'm takin' you to Frisco. Maybe you don't think much of your own life, but it don't really belong to you: it belongs to the country. What would we do if you was to be knocked off?" He glanced quickly sideways, noted the stern, hard set of Jimmy Christopher's face, and went on talking hurriedly.

"I don't care what you do to me later on, Jimmy," he said with a hint of a sob in his voice. "You can even kill me if you want."

They were closing up on the trucks ahead, and Slips put on a burst of speed, pulled up ahead of the rearmost unit in the long line. He drove in silence for perhaps fifteen minutes until he had reached the head of the column, then swung into the lead once more. Far behind him they could still hear the sharp, angry barks of the enemy cannon, and the duller, deep-throated explosions of the American trench mortars.

Jimmy Christopher sat stiffly beside McGuire. He knew that the enemy would throw every available force onto the highway in a desperate endeavor to break through the wall of resistance which the Americans were opposing now. And he knew, as well, that those Americans would fight until the last man was dead.

The trucks would have to stop for servicing pretty soon. Their speed was limited because of the unwieldiness of the column. If the enemy tanks broke through they could easily overhaul them unless the trucks had a start of at least two hours. True, they were now in American territory, but the enemy divisions could form a deep wedge to thrust in behind the American front line. It would be necessary to consolidate the American position in the Santa Rosa Mountains, to keep the Purple troops from spreading throughout Southern California.

There were many things to be done, and here Operator 5 was sitting helpless in the car.

SLIPS McGUIRE'S THOUGHTS had been running along the same lines. For he said: "Listen, Jimmy. I can't keep you tied up here all the way into Frisco. Promise me you'll come along, and not try to go back there, and I'll untie you."

"I promise!" Jimmy Christopher said curtly.

Slips drove on for a short time at a higher rate of speed than the trucks, until he attained a good lead on them. Then he pulled over to the side of the road, and busied himself with the cord about Jimmy's wrists and ankles.

In a moment Jimmy was free. Slips McGuire was looking at him like a whipped cur. "Gawd, Jimmy. Don't look at me like that. You look at me as if you hate me. I —" There was a catch in his voice —

"I only did it for your sake!"

Jimmy said hotly: "Damn you, Slips, I don't need to be wet-nursed." His lips were white with anger. "You've gone too far this time!"

White fury welled in his eyes, and he acted unthinkingly. His right fist came up in a short arc and caught Slips McGuire in the jaw. But almost as he struck, remorse gripped Operator 5. He knew that Slips McGuire would give up his life for him. There were few who were more devoted to Jimmy Christopher than was this little ex-pickpocket. What he had done he had done out of love for Jimmy Christopher. Operator 5 sought to check that blow even as he delivered it.

Instead of landing flush on McGuire's jaw, it caught him aslant. McGuire's head was thrown backward against the seat cushion. He did not raise a hand to defend himself, but merely sat there looking at Jimmy with the wide-eyed devotion of a faithful collie dog.

Jimmy Christopher was suddenly contrite. "I'm sorry, Slips," he blurted out in a swift revulsion of feeling. "I — I shouldn't have done that — I was seeing red for a minute."

Slips McGuire felt of his jaw and smiled ruefully. "That's all right, Jimmy. I deserved it. But I just couldn't see you stay there and die —"

He was interrupted by the sudden staccato voice of Z-7 coming in over the radio on the dashboard: "O-5, O-5! Your presence urgently needed in San Francisco. Reports received that Asiatic Fleet of Central Empire had destroyed Guam, Honolulu and all our Pacific defenses; San Francisco unprotected against bombardment if enemy fleet approaches. Planes our only hope of stopping enemy fleet. Gasoline must come through."

Z-7's voice dropped almost to a whisper as it changed from the formal broadcast to a more confidential tone.

"Jimmy, for God's sake, get in touch with me. Things are going all wrong here in Frisco. There's a conference of the Governors of all the Western states here and they're talking about superseding me in command of American Defense Force. I hope to heaven you get this message. I'll keep repeating it until I hear from you!"

Z-7's voice faded, and Slips McGuire exclaimed hastily: "Super-sede! Does that mean what I think it means, Jimmy? They're gonna chuck you and Z-7 out, an' try to run things themselves?"

Operator 5 nodded. "I'm afraid that's what it means, Slips. I was expecting something like this. Ever since Z-7 took charge, there's been a lot of jealousy. They can't see why they should take orders from him. The rank and file of Americans are satisfied, but it's these officials who object. Their pride is hurt."

THE TENSENESS OF A MOMENT BEFORE was forgotten by these two now, as this new emergency arose.

McGuire grated: "They'll bungle everything, the fools! They're not military men. They don't understand these things. Z-7 handled the whole Intelligence Service in the World War, didn't he? Who could do better than him? Why, if it hadn't been for you and Z-7, the Purple flag would be flying from coast to coast today!"

Operator 5 was quiet, brooding. Slips McGuire drove on for a long time in silence, while the long sinuous column of tank trucks followed. They could still hear the sounds of battle to the south, where Cahill's men were dying so that they could go on.

At last, Jimmy Christopher spoke, bitterly. "Maybe they're right, Slips. Maybe they can do better than Z-7 and I have done. Anyway, I'm tired, sick of it all. If I quit now, Diane and I could go to Mexico and settle down —"

McGuire's brittle laugh broke into his mood of dejection. "Quit? You? Hell, Jimmy, you can't quit. I won't let you quit. You've got to take this like you've taken everything else that's come along. Remember when Redfern had you scuttled? We pulled out of that, didn't we? We can pull out of this, too. Damn it, Jimmy Christopher —" there was a suspicion of tears in the little man's eyes — "you can't quit, with Cahill and those boys dying back there so we could get through. *You owe it to them to carry on!*"

Operator 5's shoulders suddenly squared. He said very low: "Of course, Slips. I owe it to them." His chin jutted, and the old fighting light came back into his eyes. "Let's go, Slips! Frisco by morning! We'll make those bureaucrats step lively to supersede us!"

Slips McGuire took a hand from the wheel to rub his jaw furtively, where Jimmy had hit him; and he grinned into the night. "Attaboy!" he said softly.

CHAPTER THREE

Betrayal

SAN FRANCISCO HAD OVERNIGHT BECOME a city of panic. The news had spread like wildfire that the great Asiatic Fleet of the Central Empire was only a thousand miles out to sea, steaming relentlessly in their direction.

Old men, women, and children swarmed on the ferries and toll bridges across the Bay, carrying their few possessions with them, and seeking refuge on the mainland in Berkeley and Oakland. Stores and offices were shut down, and everything in the city was at a standstill. There were few able-bodied men in the streets, for these were already in the front lines with the American Defense Force at the Rocky Mountains.

Those who remained here were either aged or disabled, or else were engaged in occupation necessary for the conduct of the war.

A woefully small contingent of volunteers was handling the great flow of traffic at the ferries and bridges. In Golden Gate Park thousands of people were congregated, listening avidly for the latest news of the approaching enemy fleet to be broadcast from the huge loudspeakers erected there. These were the people who had chosen not to flee from the city at the first word of danger. Most of them were old, and had lived in San Francisco all their lives. Many of them remembered vividly the great fire of 1906, and as they stood about waiting for news, they shrugged their shoulders fatalistically. "We survived that," one old man told a crony, "and we might as well stay around for what's coming now!"

Surprisingly, the panic of those who were fleeing to the mainland was not shared by these in Golden Gate Park. Many of these old men had sons and daughters in other parts of the country — east of the Rocky Mountains, where the merciless heel of the Central Empire pressed hard upon the necks of those in the occupied territory.

In the stadium in the center of the park, a quartermaster in charge of a supply company was handing out rifles to all those who wished them. Little good these weapons would do against the huge eighteen-inch guns of the Purple Fleet. But many of these oldsters were prepared to die here rather than leave the city where they had lived all their lives.

To the north of Golden Gate Park, in the Headquarters Building building of the Presidio, Z-7 sat at a desk in a small room. It was in this man's steady, capable hands that the destiny of the nation had lain for the past six months. And the strain of that responsibility wrote itself upon his face. His eyes were bloodshot from lack of sleep, and a stubble of blue-black beard showed on his unshaven cheeks.

Three other people were in that room with him — two women and a boy. The women were as unlike each other as it is possible for two human beings to be. Diane Elliot was tall, slim, almost boyish in figure, with soft, chestnut hair and vivaciously startling blue eyes. The other, Anita Monfred, was dark, with a thin face and hard black eyes. Her alluring curves were accentuated by the tight-fitting black dress she wore under her fur coat.

IN ADDITION TO BEING SO UNLIKE each other in appearance, Diane Elliot and Anita Monfred were as far apart as the poles in ideals, heredity, background, and view of life. Diane was a typical product of modern America, a young woman who had earned her living from the time she left school by entering the newspaper business and later becoming the star reporter for the Amalgamated Press.

Anita Monfred, on the other hand, though no whit less beautiful than Diane, had lived her life in the effete, unhealthy atmosphere of decadent Europe. A baroness of the Central Empire in her own right, she was first cousin to Rudolph I, the Purple Emperor. It was her cousin who was now ravishing three-quarters of America. She had been brought up in an atmosphere of conquest and cruelty. She had stood beside her cousin Rudolph while thousands of innocent Americans were executed at the Emperor's whim. Never in her life had she been unable to get what she wanted.

And now, strangely, she found herself wanting the same thing that Diane Elliot wanted — a man. That man was Operator 5. It mattered not to her that Jimmy Christopher returned Diane's affection whole-heartedly; it mattered not to her that these two were as close to each other spiritually as a man and woman can possibly be; she wanted Jimmy Christopher.

The baroness, Anita Monfred, had given up her position at the Court of Rudolph — had even caused herself to he banished and a price placed upon her head in order to aid Operator 5, and place him under obligation to her. And now, as she stood in Z-7's office, with her dark eyes fixed on Diane Elliot's beautiful countenance, a hundred emotions mingled in her breast.

The boy, Tim Donovan, was a freckle-faced lad of fifteen. For three years now he had been a hero-worshiper. The hero was Operator 5. Jimmy Christopher had taken the lad under his wing one night when the freckle-faced boy had done him a service. And ever since then the two had been almost inseparable in their adventures. Operator 5 had taught the boy to shoot, to ride, and to fly an airplane, as well as dozens of other things which the lad had grasped with an uncanny ability far beyond his years.

Now these three — the boy and the two women — were intently watching Z-7 as the latter spoke into a microphone at his desk. This microphone was connected with the short-wave radio sending outfit upstairs. He was broadcasting another message to Jimmy Christopher: "O-5! O-5! You must make better time, or you will be too late. The Board of Governors is leaving now, to ratify their act superseding me in command. Hurry!"

HE REPEATED THAT MESSAGE ONCE MORE, then arose from his desk and looked somberly at the other three. He strode past them to the window and gazed out to the east over the city. He could see the hundreds of little black dots in San Francisco Bay — the helpless, fuel-less planes which were ready to take off against the approaching Asiatic Fleet as soon as gasoline arrived. Closer to the reservation he could see the streets of San Francisco, where people were hurrying toward the ferries carrying their belongings on their backs as best they could. Z-7's brow was furrowed with anxiety, and he heaved a deep sigh.

The boy, Tim Donovan, stepped up impulsively and placed a hand on his sleeve. "Don't worry so much, Chief, things will turn out all right as soon as Jimmy gets here." The boy's small fist clenched in impotent fury. "I'd like to take these governors and knock their heads together!"

Diane Elliot came up on the other side of Z-7. She said sympathetically: "Everything is piling up at once, isn't it, Chief?"

Z-7 nodded. With a sudden access of anger he struck his clenched right fist against his open left palm. "It's this inactivity that gets me! I wish I were out doing things like Jimmy, instead of having to sit here and take all the grief. I can't understand about that Asiatic Fleet."

He swung around to face them. "I can see how those big guns of theirs could destroy our Hawaiian defenses. But why in God's name haven't we received a report from the Naval Air Base? Two dozen planes were sent out, and not one returned. Where are they? They couldn't all have gone down!"

Diane was about to speak, but Z-7 rushed on. "And that isn't all. Somewhere on this side of the Rockies, there's a traitor! Marshal Kremer knew that Jimmy was coming across the border with those tank trucks. He had advance information on it. *Someone right here in headquarters must have betrayed us!*" Z-7's piercing glance went past Diane, past Tim, and fastened on the cold, haughty face of the baroness, Anita Monfred.

She met his gaze boldly, with a scornful smile at the corners of her mouth. "Do you perhaps, accuse me of having betrayed your precious Operator 5, my friend?"

As she stood there, almost regal in her beauty, she was the epitome of feminine seductiveness. Her low-cut black dress revealed the soft white skin of her throat and bosom. Her breasts were heaving tumultuously as if she were finding it difficult to restrain her anger at the suspicion which Z-7 was directing at her.

But the stocky intelligence chief shook his head grimly. "I accuse no one, Baroness — until I have evidence. But when I have the proof, God help the traitor!"

DIANE AND TIM BREATHLESSLY watched the interplay between these two. That there was open antagonism between Z-7 and the baroness was an open secret. Z-7, in spite of the fact that his work as chief of the Intelligence dealt with cunning and intrigue and the wily schemes of unscrupulous men, was himself a blunt and forthright person. Human nature, and the things that dwelt hidden deep behind the eyes of men and women, were open books to him; and he guessed what neither Tim nor Diane suspected — namely, that the Baroness, Anita Monfred, cousin of the Purple Emperor, loved Operator 5 with a fierce, jealous passion.

He disapproved strongly of harboring her here in headquarters. "Send her back to Rudolph," he had told Operator 5 bluntly one day not so long ago.

Jimmy had refused. "Rudolph would have her executed in some particularly painful manner, Z-7," he had protested. "We can't do that to her. It would be kinder for us to shoot her."

Z-7 had shrugged. "Shoot her then. Or else send her away. Send her to Mexico. Send her to South America. Send her anywhere. But she will only make trouble if she stays here."

"Trouble?" Operator 5, keenly acute as he was in other matters, was blind to Anita's passion for him. He hadn't been able to understand what Z-7 understood only too well — that when Anita Monfred realized that Jimmy Christopher could not be lured away from Diane, the baroness would become dangerous. Z-7 had wanted to talk more frankly to Jimmy, to give him a more complete picture of the situation. But there had been so many other things of major importance demanding his attention that he had neglected to follow the matter up.

So Anita Monfred, Baroness of the Central Empire, proscribed by her own cousin the Emperor Rudolph, remained at liberty in the headquarters of the American Defense Force.

Now, whatever might have been said further by Anita and Z-7 was forestalled by an abrupt knock at the door, followed by the immediate entrance of a tall, ascetic-looking man of perhaps fifty-five. This man glanced frowningly from one to the other of the group, and pursed his lips as if in disapproval. Z-7 did not appear particularly glad to see him.

This was John Coburn, the Acting Governor of California. He had taken over the executive duties when the Governor, Lieutenant-Governor, and the entire governmental staff had volunteered to serve in the American Defense force. He walked with a slight limp in his left foot, which was deemed sufficient cause to excuse him from military service. Most of the other governors of the Western states were the same type of men — that is, those who for some reason or other could not serve in the front line against the Central Empire. It was the council of these temporary governors which was now considering taking over the active leadership of the American force.

The glances of Coburn and Z-7 locked across the room. Coburn said tightly, "Z-7, the Board of Governors of the United States, acting under my chairmanship, has arrived at its decision. You are hereby notified that you are relieved of command of the American Defense Force, to take effect immediately. When Operator 5 arrives with his gasoline trucks, he will turn them over to the officers whom we shall designate, and he will report to the Board of Governors for further orders. Kindly make arrangements to turn over all matters to me in my office within the next hour."

Z-7 flushed hotly, while Tim Donovan and Diane Elliot exchanged hopeless glances. The baroness, Anita Monfred, stood coldly at one side, listening with a supercilious smile.

The stocky Intelligence Chief exclaimed bitterly: "Look here, Coburn, you and your Board of Governors are making a terrible mistake. The only thing that has kept up the spirit of the American Defense Force is the knowledge that Jimmy Christopher is actively in charge. They have plenty of confidence in me, too, but the thing that keeps them in the front line trenches, willing, and ready to die, is the fact that they know that Operator 5 is working all the time, on his own initiative. If you take away Operator 5's authority now, I warn you, Coburn, you will shatter the morale —"

John Coburn broke in coldly: "Your opinion has not been asked, Z-7. You will merely carry out the commands of the Board of Governors!" He turned briskly and strode from the room without giving Z-7 a chance to go any further. There was a deep hush in the room as the door slammed behind the Acting Governor of California.

TIM DONOVAN GRITTED HIS TEETH and thrust his jaw out pugnaciously. "Why, that cold-livered monkey! I'd like to push his face in!"

Z-7 shrugged hopelessly. "It's no use, Tim. They're in the saddle now, and they must have their way. God help America!" His dark eyes rested on Anita Monfred. "Even if I'm only a private citizen now, Baroness, I am still looking for the traitor here in headquarters. Now that my time is my own, I'm going to spend it all in trying to find out who gave Marshal Kremer the information that Jimmy Christopher was on the way north with the gasoline trucks —"

Anita Monfred interrupted him. "I resent your suspicions, Z-7. If you have nothing definite to accuse me of —"

Tim Donovan broke in, speaking slowly. "There is something I would like to say, Baroness. I haven't spoken of it before because I didn't know if it was important. But maybe you'd like to explain to us *what you were doing last night over in the barracks where they keep the prisoners of war!*"

Anita's eyes flashed angrily.

"So you were spying on me —"

Tim Donovan's young face was clouded. "No, I wasn't spying on you. But I happened to be crossing the Presidio, and I saw you going through the alley alongside the Officers' Quarters. I didn't recognize you in the darkness, because you were dressed in a long coat. I just thought it might be somebody who didn't belong here, so I followed, and I saw you cross over to the barracks where the prisoners of war are being held.

"You stepped over to one of the barred windows, and you talked to somebody inside for about ten minutes. I was going to call the Officer of the Guard, but just then you left and started back and I saw your face, so I didn't do anything about it. But now that this question of a traitor comes up, I think you ought to explain."

Tim had spoken in a more or less casual way. Now he finished rather lamely. "I know I'm only a kid, and maybe I should have kept my mouth shut altogether. But I'd rather talk about it like this, in front of you, than come to Z-7 behind your back."

When the lad stopped talking, there was a sudden tenseness in the room. They all appreciated the significance of the revelation he had just made — Anita Monfred, a baroness of the Central Empire, stealing out under cover of darkness to hold a whispered conversation through a barred window, with a Central Empire prisoner of war!

CHAPTER FOUR

A Traitor Signals

BUT ANITA DID NOT SEEM TO BE too much disturbed by the disclosure. She frowned, apparently trying to decide just how to answer. Suddenly she appeared to reach a decision. There was a queer look in her eyes as she spoke. "Very well. It is natural that you should not trust me. I had hoped to keep this a secret until Operator 5 arrived. It was my intention to tell him about it. But since you force my hand, I must speak now."

She glanced behind her to make sure that the door was closed, then dropped her voice almost to a whisper. "You know that rumors have been coming in about the Asiatic Fleet that is now approaching San Francisco. There are rumors that the fleet vessels are equipped with some strange weapon of war that can crush all resistance. You know that the Pacific Islands have been destroyed, and you have heard that none of the planes which went out to reconnoiter that fleet have ever returned. You have been worried about that, haven't you, Z-7?"

The Chief of Intelligence nodded. "Certainly I have. But what —"

She rushed on quickly, throwing a swift side glance at Diane and Tim. "Well, my friends, there is a secret of the Asiatic Fleet. All the time that I was in the Court of Rudolph, I knew that this fleet was being built in Asia. And I knew that my cousin the Emperor, and his Minister, Baron Flexner, were gleeful about some great discovery that had been made by the Central Empire scientists. But this discovery was so shrouded in mystery that no one could guess its nature. The scientist who discovered that secret was a subject of the Central Empire by the name of Johann Vargas."

SHE STOPPED FOR BREATH, and Z-7 asked her: "What has this Johann Vargas got to do with your trip to the barracks last night? Don't tell me that we have captured Vargas without knowing it —"

She smiled and shook her head. "That would be too much good luck. But yesterday afternoon, as I passed the prisoners' barracks,

I saw the face of a man I knew in one of the windows. I stopped for a moment to talk to him, and it seemed that he had been watching for me, for the purpose of delivering a message. He insisted that I return to see him at night. Tim Donovan saw me when I came back to talk to him.

"That prisoner, my friends, deliberately allowed himself to be captured, so that he could be brought here to deliver a message either to myself or to Operator 5. That message concerns Johann Vargas. Vargas, it seems, sailed with the Asiatic Fleet, but after they destroyed Honolulu he took off in a plane and flew across to Denver at Rudolph's orders. He is now in Denver.

"Vargas was expecting a liberal reward from my cousin for developing this invention. Instead of giving him a reward, Rudolph merely thanked him in the name of the Empire. Vargas has became disgruntled and angry. He wishes to sell the secret of the Asiatic Fleet. This prisoner to whom I talked last night is his younger brother, Franz Vargas. Franz permitted himself to be captured expressly so that he could arrange for his brother to betray the Empire." The baroness drew herself up with dignity. "That, my friends, is the explanation of why I was seen stealing through the Presidio at night!" She threw a withering glance at Tim Donovan.

Z-7 stepped forward eagerly, while Diane's eyes began to sparkle with the light of sudden inspiration.

Z-7 demanded: "How — how and where is Vargas going to do this?"

"Franz Vargas told me," Anita explained, "that his brother Johann will be waiting every night this week between seven and ten o'clock, in the street in Denver directly opposite the abandoned Mint Building. He demands that he be given a plane and $50,000 in gold, and a safe conduct to any place in South America where he may desire to go. In exchange for that he will give us the secret of the Asiatic Fleet.

"Whoever comes to meet him in Denver must stand at the corner opposite the Mint Building, holding an umbrella. He will approach that person and say: *It must be raining in Asia.*' The person with the umbrella will answer: *It never rains when the fleet comes in.*' Then Vargas is to be taken to the plane and flown across the American lines. He will then drop the American emissary and continue on his way to South America where he expects to be safe from Rudolph's vengeance. He further specifies that as soon as the transaction has been completed, his brother Franz be released and sent to join him in South America."

Z-7, Tim, and Diane had listened eagerly, carefully to every word that Baroness Anita Monfred said. Now Z-7 asked her: "Why didn't you tell me about this at once? Why did you wait?"

"Because, my friend, I wished to give this information to Operator 5 personally. I was waiting for him to return."

Z-7 sighed. "It's too bad that you had to wait. Now I can't act on your information. I have to relay it to the Board of Governors. They have taken all authority from me."

Neither he nor Anita noted the tense attitude of Diane Elliot, or the calculating look in her eyes. Tim Donovan, however, was watching Diane, and a slow grin began to spread over his face, which he quickly eradicated. Diane looked at him, and a swift glance of understanding passed between the two.

Then Diane said abruptly, with a great air of casualness: "All this is very interesting. I'm sure the Board of Governors will be glad to hear of it, and will act on it with their usual efficiency. As for me, I'm getting hungry. Come on, Tim, let's go get something to eat."

She started for the door, and Tim slouched after her. "Yeah, I could eat a good mess of ham and eggs myself. See you later, Z-7. You too, Baroness."

He ambled out after Diane, but as soon as they were out of the room and the door was closed behind them, they magically lost their air of casualness and ease. Tim Donovan gripped her arm: "Are you thinking of the same thing that I'm thinking of, Di?"

She was hurrying down the corridor toward the exit, and Tim was stretching his legs to keep up with her.

"That's it, Tim. Come on, let's do this before somebody stops us." They fairly ran out of the building, and hurried over the Presidio grounds toward Crissy Field.

TIM DONOVAN PANTED: "There's a little two-seater Farnsworth-Wright monoplane on the field now, all gassed up and ready to take off. The major in charge of the field probably wouldn't know yet about the Board of Governors taking over. We'll tell the major that Z-7 is sending us on a special mission. We can take off right away, and fly across and land somewhere in Nevada. Then in the evening we can take off for Denver and meet this Vargas guy. Is that how you had it figured, Di?"

"Right, Tim. There's only one thing you forgot."

"What's that?"

"The money, Tim. Remember, he wants $50,000 in gold, and a safe conduct."

Tim stopped short in consternation. "Gee! I forgot all about that. How —"

Diane smiled. They were hurrying across the ground of Crissy Field now, for the trim, low-winged monoplane that was standing on the line ready to take off. "I know what we can do about that, too, Tim. We'll stop off at Salt Lake City. Hank Sheridan will be able to get us the gold, and he also has the authority to issue a safe conduct."

"Yeah bo!" Tim almost shouted. "That takes care of everything. Go on, Di, warm her up. I'll get our flying togs out of that locker."

While Tim ran across the field toward the locker, Diane strode with shining eyes toward the monoplane which was to carry them eastward on their adventure.But back in the Headquarters Building, neither Diane nor Tim were able to know that Anita Monfred had stared after them with a queer, inscrutable glance. A small smile quirked at her lips. She crossed the room and looked out of the window, followed there the figures of both of them as they hurried across the Presidio. Then she nodded her head almost imperceptibly.

Z-7 was watching her with a puzzled expression. "What is it, Baroness?" he asked. "Whom are you watching?"

Anita Monfred turned to him, smiling slowly, languorously. "Our two young friends," she said, "told us they were hungry. It is strange, but I did not know that there was a restaurant over at the flying field!"

Z-7 uttered a short oath and sprang across to the window. The two of them stood watching, and in a few minutes they saw the Farnsworth-Wright rise above the field and bank around to head eastward. "You think that Diane and Tim are in that plane?"

Anita Monfred let her gaze linger on him a moment, then said mockingly: "I do not think so, my friend — I am sure of it!"

AND AS THE TRIM MONOPLANE WINGED its way eastward bearing Diane and Tim toward a rendezvous with a traitor, the long column of tank trucks was making its way through San Mateo on the last lap of its long journey into San Francisco.

Jimmy Christopher and Slips McGuire drove on well ahead of the column, and went straight to Z-7's room in the Headquarters Building of the Presidio. Anita Monfred was not there when they arrived. Swiftly, Jimmy Christopher recounted to Z-7 the events of the night, which he had already relayed to him by telephone while on the road.

"You sent more troops to relieve Cahill, didn't you?" Jimmy asked.

"Yes. I ordered ten thousand men to march down from the second line of defense at Grand Canyon, and I moved a whole division in from Las Vegas. They must have passed you in the night. But I'm afraid they won't be able to hold the Purple Army back. Kremer is moving up all his heavy artillery. I'll have to take more reserves out of the second line and send them down —"

Z-7 stopped suddenly, and his shoulders drooped. "I forgot, Jimmy. I won't do any more sending. I've — I've been relieved of command! The Board of Governors under John Coburn have taken over. You're to report to them as a private operator now, not as second in command of the Defense Forces!"

Before Jimmy could say anything, Slips McGuire began to swear luridly. "Damn it! Those guys can't do that! I'm goin' out and start a revolution. I'll fix them —"

Operator 5 put a restraining hand on McGuire's arm. "Take it easy, Slips. There's plenty of trouble around as it is, without you starting more. We've got to worry about this Asiatic Fleet."

Z-7 seized the opportunity of telling Jimmy about Diane and Tim, and how they had gone without permission from the Governors to meet the traitor, Vargas. He recounted the story that Anita Monfred had told them.

Operator 5 frowned. "This secret of the Asiatic Fleet — I wonder

Operator #5

if it has any connection with the fact that our scouting planes never returned. I think perhaps we shouldn't send our planes up to try to stop the Asiatic Fleet until we know what that secret is. It would be just too bad if all these planes should be destroyed —"

He was interrupted by a knock at the door. It was John Coburn again. Coburn frowned, glancing from Z-7 to Jimmy, to Slips. "Look here, Operator 5," he rapped out. "I left instructions that you were to report to the Board of Governors as soon as you arrived."

"I'm sorry, sir," Jimmy told him. "I have just gotten in, and I'm getting the news from Z-7. We had a hard job getting the gasoline through."

Coburn nodded. "I understand that, Operator 5, and I appreciate the job you've done. We are loading the gasoline onto the planes now. We will take off this afternoon, in mass formation, to find the Asiatic Fleet and attack it. We are in hopes that we will be able to destroy the enemy's fleet —"

Jimmy Christopher interrupted him crisply. "No, no, you mustn't do that, Mr. Coburn. I'm afraid of it. I'm afraid that the Central Empire Fleet has some means of destroying our airplanes. Remember, not a single one of our scouts returned from reconnoitering the fleet. It would be disastrous if all of these planes were to be destroyed too."

Coburn sneered. "You're too timid, Operator 5. It would be impossible for such a mass formation of planes to be entirely destroyed. Please do not presume to give us your advice or your orders. We do not need it. As long as you do a good job whenever you are assigned to a task, that it all that will be expected of you from now on."

Slips McGuire's face flushed, and he was about to take an impulsive step toward Coburn, but Jimmy Christopher stopped him with a glance. "I see, sir," he said, quietly. "I will remember that."

Coburn hesitated for a moment, then turned and strode quickly from the room. At the door he swung back: "Remember, Z-7, I want everything turned over to me within the hour."

FOR A LONG TIME after acting Governor Coburn had left, there was a pregnant silence in the room. Slips McGuire was breathing heavily, barely restraining the anger he felt. Z-7 and Jimmy Christopher sat in dejected silence.

Soon Z-7 sighed and heaved to his feet. "I — I guess I better begin putting things in order, so I can turn everything over to them. I'll be seeing you later, Jimmy."

Operator 5 nodded. "Okay, Chief." He forced a smile. "Come on, Slips. We are private citizens now. Let's take a stroll through the city, and look around. In a way it's a kind of relief to be rid of all that responsibility."

Operator 5 did little the rest of that day. In silence he and Slips McGuire walked across town and climbed Telegraph Hill. From there they stood watching the great armada of planes taking off from San Francisco Bay. It was Operator 5 who had originally secured those planes, and had flown them in a brilliant attack upon the Atlantic fleet of the Central Empire. Jimmy had been forced to destroy the Panama Canal at that time in his attack upon the Central Empire's Atlantic fleet. It had been a costly but brilliant maneuver, and it had saved the United States from attack on the west coast.

Now this new menace — the mysterious Asiatic Fleet — was coming across the ocean, and these gallant aviators who had flown under Jimmy Christopher were going up again under the command of another, to face an unknown peril.

Jimmy Christopher's face was drawn and pale. "I have a feeling, Slips," he told the little ex-pickpocket, "that those men will never come back! I hope to God I'm mistaken."

They watched until the last plane had disappeared beyond the horizon to the west, and then they slowly came down from Telegraph Hill, walked across town to the Presidio. It was late in the evening when they got there, and Z-7 was waiting for them outside, in front of the Headquarters Building. He was pacing up and down impatiently, and as soon as he saw Jimmy he thrust a slip of paper into his hand.

"This came from Diane, almost an hour ago. I've been looking for you all over town. The radio operator gave it to me, rather than to the Board of Governors." He smiled grimly. "There are still some people around here who remain our friends in spite of the fact that we are not the tops any more."

Jimmy took the slip of paper, and Z-7 went on to explain: "It was transmitted from a secret amateur radio station in Denver, and our operator picked it up as best he could. There was a lot of interference. You will find some gaps in it."

Slips McGuire peered around Jimmy's shoulder as he read the message.

```
AM IN URGENT NEED OF HELP . . . CONTACTED
VARGAS, BUT WE WERE TRAPPED BY CENTRAL EMPIRE
TROOPS . . . TIM AND VARGAS ESCAPED I WAS ALMOST
CAPTURED BUT ESCAPED AND AM HIDING IN HOME OF
AMERICAN PATRIOT . . . SEND SOMEONE MEET ME
OPPOSITE MINT BUILDING BETWEEN TWO AND THREE IN
THE MORNING . . . IMPERATIVE I HAVE HELP TO FIND
TIM AND VARGAS . . . EXERT GREAT CARE AS I SUS-
PECT TRAP . . . DIANE
```

Jimmy Christopher's face was pale. Slips McGuire said under his breath, "I think you were right, Z-7. There must be a traitor somewhere in headquarters. I bet those Central Empire troopers were lying in wait for Tim and Di to meet this Vargas guy."

Z-7 went on, disregarding McGuire's comment. "I'm afraid things are pretty bad, Jimmy. The Board of Governors is doing things that you and I would never have considered. They've ordered Pike's Peak evacuated by our men. And they've sent instructions by wire for our men to plant fifty charges of explosive on the mountainside, so that when the enemy troops take possession of the peak they will be blown to bits. The explosion will be set off by radio impulse at five o'clock."

Jimmy Christopher frowned. "But that's idiotic. They ought to hold the Peak by every means possible. Those charges of explosives won't destroy the mountain, and the enemy will be able to set up guns which will command half a dozen passes in the Continental Divide. It will mean that they will be able to drive us back from the Rockies!"

Z-7 spread his hands helplessly. "It's beyond me, Jimmy. But about this message from Diane — what are you going to do?"

Jimmy's decision was already made. "Get me a plane, Z-7! Slips and I are going after them. Can you fix it so we can take off without being stopped by the Board of Governors?"

Z-7 nodded slowly. "I think I can. But we won't use Crissy Field. After Tim and Diane took off in that Farnsworth-Wright, they put a guard around the field. I'll get a car and we'll drive down to the airport at San Bruno. Major Remington over there will do anything for us. Get your things ready, and I'll phone him."

"Let's go," said Jimmy.

CHAPTER FIVE

Doom on the Heights

TWO MEN MOVED SILENTLY and furtively through the darkened streets of the city of Denver. It was two o'clock on the morning of the 240th day of the Purple Invasion of the United States. The gray-clad, goose-stepping troops of Rudolph I, Emperor of the Central Empire, Lord of Europe and Asia, had smashed their way across the country in a bloody, irresistible advance that had brought them to the foot of the Rocky Mountains.

South of Santa Fe the Purple troops had pushed even farther, crossing the Rio Grande into Arizona. But here, the natural barrier of the great Continental Divide had stopped them temporarily. The icy hand of winter had taken a seat in the grim game of war. With the mountain passes clogged by snow and ice, the American Defense Force had been able thus far to hold its ground.

But even now, as those two men stole through the city of Denver, they could hear the dull rumble of artillery to the south, where the huge Central Empire guns were pouring a terrific barrage of screaming lead against the forlorn defenders marooned on Pike's Peak. The dull reverberations of the 155 mm guns twenty miles away shook the ground upon which they trod.

The streets about them were completely deserted. Since the bloody emperor, Rudolph, had made Denver his headquarters, a strict and deadly curfew had been established. No American civilians were permitted in the streets between the hours of seven at night and seven in the morning. Death was the immediate penalty for infraction of this rule — unless a civilian could show a special permit card issued by the Commandant of the occupied territory. And neither of these men had such permit cards. In fact, there was a high price upon the head of one of them.

That one was the man who had stiffened the backbone of the American resistance to the ruthless invasion — Jimmy Christopher, known in the records of the United States Intelligence as Operator 5. It was Operator 5 who had organized the first effective stand against the war machine of the Central Empire, who had checked the advance of the Purple troops again and again, so that the campaign of conquest, which the Purple High Command had scheduled for completion by the middle of the summer, was still unfinished with winter setting in.

Jimmy Christopher had earned the undying hatred of the Emperor Rudolph by his bold counter-attacks, by the brilliant coups which he had executed during the course of the war. Now, any Central Empire officer who succeeded in bringing Operator 5 a prisoner in chains before the emperor could expect a reward beyond his fondest dreams.

Slips McGuire walked beside him.

Now, the two made their way swiftly along the dark street, wrapped in greatcoats and uniform caps taken from captured Central Empire officers. The uniforms would get them by any casual troopers, but if they should be stopped by a patrol they had no credentials to show.

SNOW CRACKLED UNDER THEIR FEET, and their breath formed clouds of steam. McGuire had his hands thrust deep into the pockets of his greatcoat, and his chin sunk into his chest. He said plaintively: "Look here, Jimmy, you're crazy to take a chance like this. You should have let me come alone. I've been here before, and I know just where to meet Diane. If they catch you, it'll be all up with the country!"

Jimmy Christopher clapped him affectionately on the shoulder. "You know you can't talk a word of the language, Slips. What would you do if a patrol stopped you?"

"I'd tell 'em I was deaf and dumb!"

Jimmy laughed, but grew serious at once, glancing back over his shoulder toward where the summit of Pike's Peak was clearly visible, illuminated by flares dropped by enemy planes which were directing the artillery fire of the Central Empire guns. "I wonder who's defending the Peak. The orders went out from Frisco to evacuate Pike's Peak. Somebody must have disobeyed orders."

Slips McGuire shrugged. "They seem to be holding out pretty well. That barrage has been going on all night. Where are we supposed to meet Diane?"

"Just about here. There are the ruins of the Mint Building. We're to wait here on the opposite corner till she shows up." Operator 5's face was set in grim lines. "She should never have come

here alone with Tim. If I had been in Frisco when she started, I wouldn't have let her go."

He stopped abruptly, stuck out a hand to grip Slips's shoulder hard. "There's a patrol coming our way, Slips! There — they've just turned the corner over there. Quick! We haven't time to get away. In this doorway!"

He pushed McGuire into the shelter of a shadow-shrouded doorway. "God grant that Diane doesn't come along at this minute. If she does . . ." his voice trailed off grimly as a heavy, blue-barreled automatic appeared in his hand.

Slips McGuire followed his example, produced an automatic. "It's dark, Jimmy. I don't think they'll spot us. As it is, we can't even see them yet. If it wasn't for their footsteps —"

He broke off. Ahead of, them, a beam of light sprang into being from the hand torch of one of the troopers in the patrol. The stream of light flickered along the street, and suddenly a shout went up from the Central Empire troopers as it silhouetted the slim figure of a young woman who was crossing the square diagonally toward the spot where Jimmy and Slips were standing. The shout of the troopers was only a dull rush of sound in the constant thunder that reverberated from the big guns shelling Pike's Peak.

But Jimmy Christopher and Slips McGuire heard it, and so did the girl. She brought up short in the middle of the street, seemingly frozen by the beam of light which limned her features clearly — strong, firm young jaw, soft lips, and abundant chestnut hair.

Operator 5 exclaimed under his breath: "Diane! They've got her!"

THE PATROL HAD BROKEN INTO A RUN, their heavy boots making the ice crackle under their feet. Diane Elliot turned to run, and the officer of the patrol called out a harsh command to halt. She kept on running, *away from the spot where she was to meet Jimmy and Slips.* She was not going to betray them!

She was wearing a light tan overcoat which flew open as she ran. Snow and sleet spattered her slender, sheer-stockinged ankles, and she almost slipped, caught her balance precariously just as a revolver in the hands of the officer barked, and a slug sang past her head. It was that slip in the snow that saved Diane Elliot's life, for it carried her out of the line of the bullet. The slug chipped cement from the corner of a building. Diane lost her balance again, sprawled in the snow. The Central Empire officer uttered a hoarse shout of triumph, leaped at her, and seized the collar of her coat, yanked her to her feet.

Diane fought him silently for a moment, then twisted out of the arms of her coat, leaving it in the officer's hands. She was revealed in a thin red dress that offered no protection against the cold blasts that whistled through the streets. She darted away from the officer, but pulled up short, her way blocked by the troopers of the patrol who had come up behind her. She turned desperately to escape, but the officer had dropped the coat and now grasped her arm.

Diane was far from giving up. She wriggled out of his grip, tried to twist away, and the officer clawed at her dress, ripping away a swath of the cloth at her shoulder. Diane's soft white flesh gleamed in the ray of the flashlight held by one of the troopers. The Central Empire soldiers surrounded her, blocking her escape. The officer laughed jarringly, and seized her wrist, twisted it behind her back. "You little spitfire!" he ejaculated. "I shall tame you!"

It was at this moment that Jimmy Christopher decided it was time to interfere. "Come on, Slips," he whispered. "We've got to bluff it through. Remember, I'm a captain, and you're a lieutenant. Act snappy, now. This is probably a non-commissioned officer, and he'll be afraid to question us!"

Thrusting the gun into his greatcoat pocket, he stepped forward out of the shadow of the doorway. Pitching his voice deep, he called out in the language of the Central Empire: "What goes on here?"

The patrol froze, but the officer did not relax his grip on Diane. He had been in the shadow all of this time, for the flashlight had not touched him. Now he spoke a quick command, and the trooper turned the beam on Jimmy and Slips. Diane Elliot allowed a slight gasp to escape her, but beyond that she gave no sign that she had recognized them. The officer asked suspiciously: "Who are you?"

Jimmy stepped closer, staring into the light. He said crisply: "Tell your man to turn that light the other way. What do you mean by questioning your superior officer?"

The patrol commander grunted. "Superior officer?" He spoke to the trooper: "Turn the light upon *me,* Carl, so that the gentleman may see whom he addresses!"

The trooper obeyed, and Jimmy restrained a start of surprise. This was no non-commissioned officer he was addressing. The light played on the gold ornaments on the man's collar — the crossed broadswords and the severed head, with two gold bars beneath. *The patrol officer was a Colonel of the Guard!*

Jimmy Christopher heard the sharp intake of breath from Slips McGuire, close behind him, and then the voice of the colonel: *"Stand at attention, Captain — and you, Lieutenant.* You will explain what you are doing here tonight!"

The trooper had swung the beam of light back to Jimmy and Slips, and the colonel was holding tightly to Diane's wrist. "Quickly!" the colonel barked. "You will give your names and regiments!"

The colonel's gun was out, in his left hand, and the rifles of the four troopers of the patrol were lowered significantly, with the muzzles glaring at them. Jimmy wondered swiftly what had brought a colonel of the Guard out here on patrol duty at this hour of night. He had neatly walked into as pretty a trap as anybody could have planned. With a non-commissioned officer, he might have had some chance of bluffing him into turning Diane Elliot over to him: now, there was little chance of safety for himself or Slips.

But while his thoughts were racing over possibilities of escape, he was saying smoothly: "Captain Schlemmer and Lieutenant Wagner, of the Forty-eighth Imperial Infantry, *Herr* Colonel. We —"

"You lie!" the colonel barked. "You wear the uniforms of the Forty-eighth Imperial Infantry, but that regiment has gone south. You are spies. *Shoot them down, men!"*

THE COLONEL'S GUN SPAT FLAME as he squeezed the trigger. But Diane, with her quick intuition, had sensed that the officer was about to shoot, and she threw herself against him, deflecting his aim. The bullet *spatted* harmlessly into the ground, just as the four troopers raised rifles to shoulder.

Jimmy Christopher's gun came out of his greatcoat pocket, and vomited thunder and fire. He shot with quick, deadly precision, picking off the troopers one after the other. From just behind him Slips McGuire's automatic spat spitefully in cackling accompaniment to Operator 5's heavier weapon.

Two troopers fell in that first blast, and the other two shot their rifles in hasty panic, the shots going wild. The Central Empire officer was struggling with Diane, who had grasped his gun arm, and was clutching his wrist desperately to her breast. The officer had twisted about in such fashion as to place her between himself and Jimmy's flashing gun.

The two troopers who were unhurt dropped to one knee, triggering their rifles wildly. Jimmy Christopher did not move front where he stood, firing coolly, methodically. He placed two shots accurately between the eyes of each of the troopers, and the men fell, leaving their officer standing alone, facing Jimmy and Slips, protected from their fire by the body of Diane. But Diane Elliot was clinging to his gun hand with obstinate perseverance. The officer relaxed his grip on her arm, raised his clenched fist and brought it down in a savage blow against her temple.

The blow did not render her unconscious, but she reeled, and her grip on the officer's wrist fell away. He lunged backward, crouching, and raising the gun. But he had no chance to shoot, for Jimmy Christopher had launched himself through the air, his powerful body forming a veritable catapult that crashed into the other, smashing him down. The officer uttered a howl of rage, squirmed out from under Jimmy, and raised his gun.

Operator 5 seized his wrist and twisted, just as the man pulled the trigger. The muzzle of the gun was deflected toward the officer's throat as it exploded. Smoke and powder filled Jimmy Christopher's eyes and lungs, and his ears were deafened by the thunderous explosion close to his cheek. The struggling form of the Central Empire officer suddenly went limp under him, and Operator 5 got slowly to his feet, looking down grimly at the raw, torn, bleeding throat of the colonel. The heavy slug had torn away the whole front of the man's neck.

Slips McGuire was busily slipping a new clip in his automatic.

"Boy!" he said earnestly. *"That* was action!"

Diane Elliot stood swaying dizzily, still numbed by that blow on the temple. Blood from the wounds of the dead troopers and their officer was staining the snow a sickish scarlet. Still the distant cannonading drummed insistently through the night in a macabre undertone. The fight had been short, swift and vicious. No doubt there were other patrols in the neighborhood, that might have heard the shooting, might even now be hurrying toward them on the double-quick.

Jimmy Christopher listened intently for a moment, then swiftly swung toward McGuire. "We've got to get out of here quick, Slips. As soon as these bodies are found, the city'll be too hot to hold us. Let's go!"

He snatched up Diane's coat, and threw it around her shoulders. She was shivering with the cold, and her lips were blue. Gratefully she slipped her arms into the sleeves, wrapped it around her. "Jimmy — I — this patrol — it was looking for me. That's Colonel Brock. He took the patrol out himself. . . . They died so quickly —"

JIMMY CHRISTOPHER PUT HIS ARM around her, pressed her close. In his eyes there was a deep admiration for this courageous girl who insisted on risking her life every minute of the day, because she knew that he too kept thrusting his head into danger. The affection between these two was a thing much deeper than the love of a man for a woman. It was founded on mutual respect, admiration, a full understanding by each of the qualities of the other. And if Diane Elliot seemed to thrust herself recklessly into danger, Jimmy Christopher understood that it was because she needed just such a powerful anodyne to drive from her heart the wistful thoughts of a happiness that could not be; for as long as their country was in danger, there could be no such thing as the quiet content of marriage and a home for the man who was known as Operator 5 or for the girl who loved him.

Even their rare moments of meeting were snatched, like this one, from the very jaws of death, with peril ever at their elbows. Now, he threw her a quick smile. "Don't let it get you, Di. This is war. It was their life or ours." He was urging her back along the way they had come, toward the outskirts of the city, while Slips

McGuire prowled behind them, gun in hand, on the watch for possible pursuit.

They turned a corner, followed a narrow street west, then turned another corner. Slips McGuire came up abreast of them, grinned in the dark, and pocketed his automatic. "I guess we're okay now, Jimmy. By the time another patrol finds those corpses, they won't know which way we went."

For answer, Jimmy Christopher silently pointed to the hard crust of snow lying on the street. Looking backward, Slips whistled. "Gawd! I never gave it a thought!"

Their three sets of footprints lay in the snow behind them as plainly as if they had left a message indicating what direction they had taken. "No, Slips," Operator 5 told him. "We won't be safe till we get out of Denver."

He led the way swiftly, in silence, for perhaps ten minutes. He turned left into an alley, and Diane uttered a gasp of surprise at sight of the grey staff car bearing the insignia of the Central Empire. Jimmy laughed. "How do you like our getaway car, Di? We stole it from the Imperial parking place in front of Rudolph's headquarters. It ought to get us out of town anyway."

Jimmy Christopher slid behind the wheel of the staff car, and Slips McGuire got in beside him. Diane crouched in the rear where she would not be seen.

Jimmy drove at a sedate pace through the dark city, being cautious not to arouse suspicion by driving too fast. Twice they passed Central Empire patrols, and the non-commissioned officers stopped them to inquire whether they had seen any suspicious characters. It appeared that the dead bodies of the Colonel and the troopers had already been discovered, and the city was being scoured for the attackers. But in both cases they were more fortunate than in their first encounter, for the non-commissioned officers of the Central Empire had a healthy respect for the captain's uniform Operator 5 wore.

They passed out of the city safely and progressed without any interference until they swung into the highway leading to Colorado Springs. Here the road was filled with slowly moving troops, consisting of infantry, artillery caissons, and supply and ammunition wagons. At sight of the staff car, however, a way was cleared

for them to pass.

Slips McGuire nudged Jimmy Christopher. "Gawd, Jimmy! They're moving all these troops down toward Pike's Peak. When the barrage lifts, I think they're going to charge. Whoever is up

there won't make out so good!"

Diane tugged frantically at his coat. "Jimmy! We've got to think of something! We've got to save them!"

Slips McGuire laughed hollowly. "Swell chance we've got! It's bad enough getting to the top of that skyscraper of a mountain without going through shellfire. No one could go through that barrage and live!"

Jimmy Christopher's eyes were studying the countryside as he guided the car along the mountainous road. They should be near Colorado Springs, or near the road leading westward through Ute Pass toward Trout Creek Pass. Pike's Peak was very close now, towering immensely above them. The artillery fire, he judged, was coming from batteries located somewhere east of Colorado Springs.

Operator 5 followed the narrow ribbon of road alongside the

moving troops. His eyes were fixed toward the southwest where the tall, stately pile of Pike's Peak loomed high above them in the night, made ghastly by the fitful light of flares and by the bursting of exploding shells.

"We'll cut across toward Trout Creek Pass," he told Slips, "and get away from these troops." His lips formed a tight, grim line. "Whoever is up there on the Peak has disobeyed orders. Pike's Peak was ordered evacuated last night. They've planted charges of high explosives in fifty places on the mountainside. They are going to wait until five o'clock in the morning, and then set that explosive off by radio impulse. They figured that the Central Empire troops would be occupying Pike's Peak by five o'clock. Now, whoever is up there will go sky high."

Operator 5 laughed bitterly. "By defending the Peak against the Purple troops, they're committing suicide!"

"My Gawd, Jimmy!" Slips McGuire exclaimed, "I clean forgot about that! Let's cut as far away from the Peak as we can!"

Abruptly, Diane Elliot's head rose in the rear of the car, close to Operator 5's shoulder. "No, no, Jimmy!" she blurted. "We've got to go to Pike's Peak! *Tim Donovan is there, and I think he has the secret of the fleet that's coming from the East!*"

CHAPTER SIX

Into the Fire

IF ONE OF THOSE SHELLS being hurled from the enemy's 155 mm guns had suddenly burst in the road directly in front of their car, the shock could not have been greater than Diane's announcement.

Slips McGuire stiffened in his seat, and exclaimed; "Tim Donovan — up there!"

Jimmy Christopher tautened and the blood drained from his face. His knuckles whitened as his hand increased the tension of its grip on the wheel. He held the car steady on the road, and stared straight ahead.

"Why didn't you tell me before?" he asked huskily. "Why did Tim go up there?"

Diane's lips were quivering. She was on her knees now, her head raised in full view of the troops they were passing, utterly forgetful of her danger.

"I — something must have happened to me when that colonel hit met on the head. I've been dazed — I haven't been able to collect my thoughts. Just now, looking toward the Peak, it all came back to me.

"You know Tim and I flew here to buy the secret of the Fleet from a traitor. Tim waited with the plane in a field just off the Salida Road where we had landed. I walked into Denver and met our man. We were going back to the plane where we had left Tim.

"But on the way, I was recognized by Colonel Brock — the man you killed back there. He had seen me at the siege of Phoenix last week, and he remembered me. He would have arrested us both, but I ran and led him away from the traitor."

Slips McGuire drew in a quick breath. "You mean you drew off the chase so this other guy could get away and go to meet Tim."

"Yes, Slips. My own life didn't matter, as long as we got that secret." She paused, then went on. "Fortunately, I got away in the darkness, and found an open doorway. It was the home of a patriotic American civilian. He gave me shelter, and his son sent you that message on his amateur radio. I stayed there until it was time to come out and meet you.

"But earlier in the evening, before curfew time, my host had gone out and listened to the gossip in the street. He came back and reported that the traitor, Johann Vargas, had reached the plane, but that they hadn't been able to take off. Tim and Vargas commandeered a motorcycle and headed South. They met a force of Americans who were reconnoitering, but their retreat was cut off by the Central Empire troops. Tim and Vargas and the other Americans were forced to take refuge at the Peak."

A sob caught in her throat. "They've been shelling Pike's Peak all night!"

Jimmy Christopher glanced at his wrist watch. It was four o'clock.

"One hour," he muttered, "and they'll all go sky-high!"

Ahead of them, a cross-road came into view. The troops were moving into position on both sides of the road here, but the artillery kept on along the same road. It was apparent that the infantry was being concentrated for the attack on Pike's Peak as soon as the gun fire ceased. Slips McGuire was peering ahead. His face was drawn and white as he looked up toward the Peak. "Gawd," he muttered. "I wonder could anything still be alive up there."

Diane broke in hastily. "There's only an hour to go, Jimmy. What will we do?"

"We're going up there!" Jimmy said tightly. "Even if Tim Donovan weren't up there, we've got to get that Vargas man back to Frisco with his secret!"

THEY WERE DRIVING UNDER THE SHADOW of the mountains now, within sight of Ute Pass. The road to Pike's Peak lay straight ahead, and wherever they looked they saw massed troops of infantry. The din of the barrage had become so intensified that they could barely hear themselves speak, even when they shouted. They could see Peak's Pike clearly, and could make out the tracks of the cog-wheel railway car, which ran straight up toward the summit. Bright beams of light illuminated the mountainside, showing them that the enemy's artillerymen had placed their shots carefully, so as not to injure the cog-railway track or the macadam automobile road which wound to the top. They were preserving a means of approach for themselves when the barrage

JIMMY CHRISTOPHER

should be lifted.

Diane was silent now, crouching in the rear of the staff car, out of sight. Jimmy Christopher drove straight ahead, and the insignia on the staff car opened the way for him. He shouted to Slips, over the thunder of the gunfire: "There's the front line, preparing to advance. The barrage must be scheduled to cease almost at once. God, if we only had some credentials, or something that would get us past the front lines —"

Slips McGuire looked sheepish. "How would you like to have the credentials of a colonel of the Imperial Guard?" he asked modestly. In his long, slender fingers there suddenly appeared a black leather folder. He slipped it open to show the Imperial insignia of the Central Empire stamped upon a card bearing the commission of Colonel Brock. Jimmy Christopher tore his eyes from the road for the moment, and glanced at it. He swore softly under his breath. "You son-of-a-gun ! Up to your old tricks!"

Slips McGuire shrugged. "Once a pickpocket, always a pickpocket. While you were talking to Di, I went through the colonel's pockets. I figured you might need something like this!"

Jimmy Christopher put his hand on McGuire's knee, and pressed it affectionately. "That commission will be a lifesaver, Slips," he said. He took the leather folder and slipped it into the pocket of his own coat. Then he drove on toward the foot of the mountain.

Diane, in the rear, asked eagerly: "Jimmy! You're going to drive up to the top?"

He nodded. "We'll drive right past the front line, and go up. Remember, Slips; I'm Colonel Brock of the Imperial Guard, if we should be questioned."

Slips McGuire shook his head dubiously. "That'll get us up all right, but what'll we do when we're up there, and how will we get down?"

At that moment, a sudden dreadful hush descended upon the whole area. For a moment it seemed as if the world had stopped moving. The barrage had ceased.

Small noises became large. They could almost feel their eardrums distending from the abrupt silence. The noise of their motor sounded like giant thunder.

A VERY FLARE GUN WAS FIRED fired somewhere to the east, and then whistles began to blow. It was zero hour. The enemy was about to advance. Gray-clad infantry debouched towards the foot of the mountain.

Jimmy Christopher pressed his finger on the button of the horn, and drove straight ahead past the first contingent of the advancing troops. A Central Empire captain was leading these troops, with a gun in one hand, and a whistle in the other. He glanced around as the raucous notes of Jimmy's horn shrilled behind him, and stepped into the path, raising a hand.

Operator 5's eyes narrowed. Straight ahead, past the captain, lay the concrete automobile road, winding up toward the summit of the mountain. He could run this man down, of course, but even though this was war such a procedure was alien to his instincts. Besides, the advancing troops would immediately turn machine guns and rifles upon the car.

Jimmy braked the car to a stop, and the officer stepped alongside. Jimmy had previously torn the epaulettes from the shoulders of his coat, and he noted that the Central Empire captain wore no epaulettes either. Officers generally did this in an engagement, to prevent the enemy from picking them off.

The Central Empire captain was looking quizzically at the insignia on the staff car, and he said firmly: "You will have to remain behind, sir. No one is permitted to precede the advance troops."

Jimmy Christopher flipped open the black leather case that Slips McGuire had given him, and exhibited the identifying credentials. "I am Colonel Brock of the Imperial Guard. At His Majesty's command I am going up first."

The Central Empire captain's eyes narrowed, and he said: *"Colonel Brock!* I know Colonel Brock well. You're not he!" The Captain's eyes were glittering with excitement. "You are a spy —"

He raised his gun and pointed it at Jimmy, his finger contracting on the trigger.

But before he could fire, there was the flash of an explosion from alongside Operator 5, and a slug sizzled past Jimmy Christopher to bury itself in the Central Empire captain's forehead. Slips McGuire had fired with the speed of light.

The Captain was flung backward into the ditch, his hands outstretched, the gun and whistle dropping to the ground.

Operator 5 rapped out: "Thanks, Slips. That was close!" He slammed the gear shift into first, and stepped down on the accelerator, racing the car up the steep incline past the moving troops.

Cries and shouts went up from all around them, but none of the

Central Empire soldiers knew exactly what had happened. They had seen the captain fall, but some of the defenders of the Peak were firing down at them from up above, and they thought that he had been hit by the American gun fire. Other men were falling about them, and it was natural to assume that this had been the case. Also, they were not suspicious of the staff car, as their captain had been.

In a moment Jimmy Christopher had pulled the car far out ahead of the leading troops, in a mad race up the automobile road. Not far away they could see the standard-gauge tracks of the cogwheel railway which in peace times took tourists to the top of the mountain.

And now rifle and machine gun bullets *spanged* into the front of the car, forming myriads of criss-cross cracks in the shatter-proof windshield.

APPARENTLY SOME OF THE DEFENDERS of the summit of the mountain were still alive after that dreadful barrage. Slips McGuire exclaimed: "Say, Jimmy! Those guys up there think we're the enemy. If they keep on shooting at us we'll never reach the top —"

"I'll fix that —" Operator 5 said — "if Tim Donovan is still alive." He began to press his fingers on the horn button in quick, sharp jabs, some long, some short.

Diane, who had been silent in the rear all this time, now leaned eagerly forward. "The code, Jimmy! You're sending Tim a message!"

Operator 5 was doing just that. Long ago, he had seen to it that Tim Donovan, as well as Diane and Slips, made themselves thoroughly familiar with the International Code. Any of them could send or receive a message in this way, and on many an occasion in the past this knowledge of the code had saved the day for them.

Now, Operator 5 kept tapping out the code signal for Tim Donovan's initials: Long, long, short, short "T. D., T. D."

He repeated the code signal half a dozen times as he guided the car in its mad dash up the winding automobile road. Then he shrugged, said to Slips McGuire and Diane: "I'll have to take a chance on Tim's having caught the signal." He began tapping out a message on the auto horn. *"Cease firing, Tim. Diane, Slips, and I are in staff car. Let us through. O-5."*

As soon as he had finished, he repeated the message, while Diane and Slips waited eagerly for some sign that the communication had been heard by those above. He began on the third repetition, and Diane whispered breathlessly: "If Tim is dead —"

And just then, with the abruptness of lightning, the firing from above ceased!

"He caught it! He caught it!" Slips McGuire shouted jubilantly.

A grim smile hovered about the corners of Jimmy Christopher's mouth. He did not lift his foot from the accelerator of the car, as he twisted it now to the right, now to the left, to follow the mountain road. The fourteen-thousand-foot climb was a trying test for the car, and time was growing precious. Jimmy Christopher's wrist watch showed four-thirty. In half an hour the explosives planted on the mountainside would be detonated.

They were almost in sight of the summit. But how they were to get down again was an open question, unspoken, in the minds of all three of them. Diane peered out of the rear window and saw far below, and indistinct in the night, the moving figures of the massed Central Empire Infantry, crawling inexorably upward along the automobile path as well as along the right-of-way of the cog railway. Those men would effectively block their descent.

CHAPTER SEVEN

The Fall of Pike's Peak

NOW THE AIR HAD GROWN colder, crisper, and sharper. It was lighter up here, too, and peering ahead once more over Jimmy's shoulder, Diane could discern the deeply-mowed furrows in the mountain side where the huge enemy shells had been dropping all night. The face of the mountain was pitted and scarred as if the earth were suffering from some virulent disease. In the gray cold light of the early dawn they could see torn and maimed bodies lying everywhere — the bodies of the American defenders who had perished under the dreadful artillery barrage of the enemy. The horror and the pity of it all struck her like a visible blow. War! Why must men make war? Why must men be cursed with violent ambitions to rule and conquer their fellow-men — why must mankind destroy itself like this?

Her face was white, and her lips quivered. She was a woman, and she loved the man in front of her at the wheel of the car. But that love would forever be denied — because there were such things in the world as stupidity, and ambition, and ruthlessness, and a heady love of power!

A sharp exclamation escaped from Slips McGuire. They had reached the summit, and as Jimmy Christopher allowed the staff car to come to a halt, they could see the hulk of the cog-railway car with its little engine, parked on the tracks. It had been carefully spared by the enemy's fire, for the Central Empire High Command no doubt realized that the engine and the tracks would be valuable to them as a means of bringing heavy artillery to the top of the mountain once they had captured it. Now, as Jimmy, Slips, and Diane emerged from the staff car, they were greeted by a shout, and half a dozen ragged, tattered, begrimed, and black-faced individuals ran out from under the shelter of the car. Among them was the slight, slim figure of Tim Donovan. The lad uttered a shout of joy and fairly leaped toward them, gripping Jimmy Christopher's hand and shaking it wildly.

The other Americans crowded around them, hurling questions at them, clawing at them, and patting them on the back.

Tim Donovan swung on Diane: "Di! Why did you bring them up

here? Now we're all trapped! There's no way of getting down. Look at those troops. They'll be up here in no time!"

Jimmy Christopher glanced around at the scores of dead, broken, and maimed bodies lying all around them. There were several emplacements for big guns, but all that remained of them now was a tangled mass of wreckage. Here and there little triangular flags fluttered on short poles. They marked the spots where the high explosives had been buried. The enemy shellfire had failed to reach these charges because they had been sunk very deep.

"If we could only find the antenna wires —"

"What do you mean?" Tim broke in.

Jimmy told him grimly: "It's exactly four-forty, Tim. At five o'clock this whole mountain is going to go up in the biggest explosion you've ever seen. It's all mined. And they're going to explode it by a radio impulse. If we don't find the antenna, it'll be all over with Pike's Peak — and with us!"

The ragged Americans who had come forward with Tim crowded around them. Sudden anxiety swept through the tattered heroes who had defended the mountain. They had been through a hell of an artillery barrage for a whole night, but the thought of being blown to bits in an explosion caused them to shudder.

Slips McGuire said bitterly: "You picked a fine time to come up here, Tim. What was the big idea?"

Diane Elliot stepped forward impulsively, put her hand on Jim Donovan's arm. "Tim! Is Vargas here? I don't see him. Is he — dead?"

Tim Donovan regarded her somberly "He is wounded, Di. We carried him into the observation car — that was the only safe place on the mountain all night. The enemy must be saving that car for something. They didn't drop a single shell on it or on the track."

Suddenly, wild shouts were heard from below. Machine guns began to chatter. The foremost of the advancing Central Empire troops were close to the summit. Bullets began to whine among them, and one of the Americans abruptly threw up his hands and fell prone on the ground, quivered and lay still. Another and another fell, and the hard-pressed group retreated quickly before the machine-gun fire of the attacking enemy. They reached the cog-wheel railway car, and Jimmy Christopher shouted: "Everybody in! We're going away from here!"

Diane asked: "Jimmy — what —"

He didn't answer, but pushed her in, waited until the last of the Americans was inside the car, then leaped up into the engine. Shots were spattering against the sides of the observation car as well as of the engine now, and Jimmy Christopher seized the wheel that controlled the brakes, spun it, and the engine began to creak and slowly move down along the tracks.

Tim Donovan came running out into the engine and shouted: "Yeah bo! We're going through them!"

THE ENGINE BEGAN TO ROCK and quiver as it gained speed down the steep tracks. Ahead of them they could see the figures of the masked infantry of the enemy, pushing steadily along the right of way of the tracks. They were heading right down into that throng of soldiers. Now they were being subjected to a concentrated fire from rifles and machine guns, and the clanging of the slugs against the metal sides and front of the engine beat a wild and deadly tattoo of death. As the figures of the troops on the right of way rushed up toward them with incredible speed, Tim Donovan swung out into the cab with a submachine gun which he handed to Jimmy Christopher.

It was high time.

Diane pointed frantically toward the right, where some of the troopers were hastily wheeling a half dozen motorcycles over toward the tracks. Their intention was clear. They were going to place those motorcycles across the tracks so that the cog-wheel railway car would strike them full on. Any such obstruction that they might hit at the speed at which they were going would certainly wreck them.

Jimmy Christopher raised the submachine gun grimly and sent a spatter of lead in the direction of those troopers. They dropped the motorcycles and scampered for cover. Beside him, Diane was firing a rifle at another group of soldiers who were trying to dislodge a huge rock which would fall in their path as soon as it was started rolling. Her accurate shooting dropped two of those soldiers, and the rest desisted quickly.

Now the car had raced into the thick of the soldiers, and they leaped frantically aside in order to escape the juggernaut of death.

They plowed through that mass of Purple infantry, crushing many of the soldiers who had failed to get out of their way quickly enough, hurling bodies to the right and left of the tracks.

Sudden consternation seized the Purple troops, and they fled from the track all the way down the line. The way was suddenly cleared to the bottom of the mountain. Jimmy Christopher started to brake the engine in order to slow up before it reached the bottom. Tim Donovan picked up the submachine gun which he had laid aside, and kept on sending burst after burst at the attacking troops.

As they slowed down at the bottom of the mountain, the Americans in the car behind piled out, with rifles, grenades, and two submachine guns. A withering fire met them from several companies of Central Empire troops concentrated on the road opposite. The men fell before they could fire a shot.

Jimmy Christopher hurried back into the observation car and found a man in the uniform of the Central Empire lying on the floor of the car. There was a crude bandage around his chest, and his head had been propped up by a pillow. Tim Donovan came in beside Operator 5 and said "This is Vargas, Jimmy. What'll we do —"

Jimmy Christopher bent down without hesitation and seized the man under the arms, raised him up and slung him over his shoulder. Vargas groaned, moaned weakly: "Don't move me. Don't move me. I'm bleeding again. I'll die —"

"Sorry," Jimmy Christopher muttered. "You'll have to take your chances on that. If I leave you here your own troops will shoot you as a traitor."

He swung out of the observation car onto the ground to stand facing a Central Empire lieutenant who was in command of the Purple troops that had surrounded the observation car. The lieutenant, seeing Jimmy's uniform, hesitated, and saluted crisply; then looked at the bleeding figure of Vargas on Jimmy's shoulder.

Operator 5 spoke with a gruff assumption of authority: "Lieutenant! Move all the troops down from the mountainside at once! The entire mountain is mined. It will be destroyed within five minutes."

The lieutenant glanced from Jimmy to Diane and Tim, who had leaped down beside him. He had seen the cog-wheel railway car coming down the mountainside, had seen the burst of fire as they had shot at the Central Empire troops.

MANIFESTLY, HE WAS IN DOUBT as to just what to do.

"These people —" he indicated Diane and Tim — "we have been searching for them, sir. And that is Vargas whom you have on your shoulder —"

Jimmy Christopher nodded. "All that is true, lieutenant. I am an officer of his Imperial Majesty's guard —" Jimmy was careful not to give the name of Colonel Brock this time lest the lieutenant also recognize him as an imposter. "But please do not delay here. I assure you the mountain will be dynamited within the next five minutes!"

The lieutenant was plainly skeptical. The conversation had been conducted in the language of the Central Empire, and now from the observation car behind Jimmy came the voice of Slips McGuire: "I've got that punk covered, Jimmy. Say the word and I'll nail him between the eyes!"

Just then a non-commissioned officer of the Central Empire sidled up to the lieutenant and whispered in his ear. The man's voice was harsh, and the words carried to Jimmy. He was telling the lieutenant that this was the officer in the staff car that had raced through the troops. As the man continued, the lieutenant's eyes widened, and he uttered a short guttural oath.

"You are no Central Empire officer!" he exclaimed. "You are a spy in league with this woman and the boy, and the traitor, Vargas. You —"

His subsequent words were never uttered. A thunderous detonation like the concentrated concussion of a thousand thunderbolts suddenly smashed at their eardrums, shook the ground beneath them, and hurled them from their feet. The whole side of the mountain seemed to rise into the air as if propelled by hands of angry giants beneath the earth. The Central Empire troops, who had not heard Jimmy Christopher's warning to the lieutenant, were taken completely by surprise. The force of the explosion left not a single man standing.

And from above them a veritable landslide of earth and rock and the bloody remnants of human beings came hurtling down toward them. In a moment they would be engulfed by the immense, sliding cataract of debris. The lieutenant was on his knees now, frantically fumbling around on the ground for the gun which he had dropped, his bloodshot eyes fixed on Jimmy's small group.

Jimmy Christopher sprang to his feet and found Slips McGuire scrambling up on the ground beside him. Slips had been hurled bodily from the observation car. Diane and Tim were also getting up, a bit dazed, and Tim Donovan shamefacedly put a hand over his face to conceal the fact that the concussion had given him a severe case of nosebleed. Slips McGuire, on his hands and knees, saw the lieutenant picking up his gun from the ground, and launched himself through the air to smash into the Central Empire officer. The lieutenant dropped his gun and grappled with Slips.

The shower of wreckage and debris had reached close to the foot of the mountain now, with an ever-increasing roar of thunder. Jimmy Christopher sprang to Slips McGuire's assistance, and brought a hard, bunched fist up in an arcing blow to the lieutenant's jaw. The officer dropped like a log, and Jimmy leaped back without waiting to see him fall, stooped, and seized the inert form of the traitor, Vargas, lifted him once more across his shoulder and shouted to the others: "Let's go!"

Closely bunched, the small group consisting of Jimmy with Vargas on his shoulder, Diane, Tim, and Slips — the only ones left alive of the group that had come down in the cog-wheel railway car — sped away from the impending doom of the landslide.

The Central Empire troops were too panic-stricken to pay attention to anything. Officers as well as men were fleeing from the crumbling mountain.

Jimmy Christopher led the way off the road toward the west in the direction of Ute Pass.

DOWN HERE IT WAS MUCH DARKER than it had been at the top of the mountain. The figures of the wildly scrambling Central Empire troops were merely shadows in the blackness. Behind them the tortured mountain was dully rumbling as huge rocks gained momentum in the devastating landslide. Enemy planes were rushing toward the mountain, dropping flares in an effort to discover just what had happened. The night was wild with confusion and panic.

And through it all the small band of fugitives pushed steadily westward through ankle-deep snow toward Ute Pass.

Operator 5 led the way carrying the limp form of Vargas, which was proving to be more and more of a burden as the snow grew deeper. Behind him trudged Diane and Slips, with Tim Donovan bringing up the rear. Behind them, grim catastrophe rode the mountainside of Pike's Peak. Thousands of Central Empire troops had perished in the cataclysmic explosion. Though it was not a major disaster to the Central Empire, it served the purpose of throwing the Purple troops into utter confusion, and thus aiding the escape of Jimmy Christopher and his band.

But their escape was not yet assured. They came in sight of the Federal Highway which led from Colorado Springs to Trout Creek Pass. Ahead of them lay Ute Pass through which they had to make their way in order to cross the mountains. If they could only reach Ute, they would be safe, for the Central Empire troops had not yet moved in that direction. Ute Pass was being held by the Americans, and it was apparent that the Purple High Command had been so anxious to capture Pike's Peak because of the fact that from the Peak they could command Ute as well as Trout Creek Pass. Though it would be impossible for the enemy to cross the mountains in the face of the Americans' defense of these passes, Marshall Kremer, the Commander-in-chief of the Purple army, no doubt felt that the Americans would retreat from these passes under a steady bombardment from Pike's Peak.

Jimmy Christopher staggered tinder the load of the moaning Vargas. The traitor was bleeding freely, and the deep snow behind them showed a trail of deep red.

Suddenly Slips McGuire called out to Operator 5: "Jimmy! I think Vargas is dead!"

Jimmy Christopher stopped, and carefully swung Vargas down, laid him on his back in the snow. Vargas's eyes were closed, and there seemed to be no cloud on his breath. The man lay still, unmoving, with his bloody chest almost entirely exposed by the fallen bandage.

Shadowy figures of enemy troops were moving all about them, and Slips McGuire kept anxious watch, gun in hand, in case they should be approached.

Jimmy Christopher bent his head low, close to that of the traitor. "Vargas!" he exclaimed. "Open your eyes, man!"

His finger on Vargas's pulse told him that the man was not yet dead. He looked up as Diane knelt beside him. "If we could only make him talk! A little brandy —"

From behind him, a scrawny hand was thrust out, clutching a small pint hip flask. He looked up into the sheepish face of Slips McGuire.

Slips lowered his eyes before Jimmy's reproving glance. "I — I couldn't help it, Jimmy. I found it in the inside pocket of Colonel Brock's coat. See, it's almost full, and it looked like an awful shame to leave it with a dead man. He didn't need it any more."

Jimmy Christopher's mouth quirked at the corners but he immediately repressed the smile, and shook his head frowningly. "Will you never reform, Slips?" he asked. But at the same moment he took the flask, unscrewed it, and forced apart the lips of the pallid-faced Vargas. He poured some of the liquor into the man's mouth, and Vargas choked, gagged, then swallowed. They could almost see the fiery brandy coursing through the man's body, Suddenly his eyes jerked open, and his lips moved. He was speaking incoherently.

Diane moaned: "He's delirious! He'll die without talking!"

Jimmy's hands were bloody from contact with the man's chest. He lifted Vargas's head, poured some more brandy between his teeth, muttering: "I hate to do this to you, old man, but it's war!" He watched Vargas carefully as the liquor brought a slight spark of life to the eyes.

"What's the secret of the Asiatic fleet!" Operator 5 demanded tensely, with his lips close to the traitor's ear.

Vargas's eyes blinked feebly, and words rushed from his lips in a torrent in the guttural language of the Central Empire "The fleet! The Asiatic fleet! The great sea fleet of Rudolph! I hate Rudolph! I will betray him!"

"Yes, yes," Jimmy Christopher said gently. "That's right, old man. What about the Asiatic fleet?"

The traitor's voice rose in a shrill, delirious cackle. "The Fleet! Ha, ha! When I sell the secret of the fleet to the Americans, I will laugh at Rudolph. Much gold and a safe conduct to South America. I will make them give me that. Ha, ha!"

"What about that fleet, man?" Operator 5 demanded. "What's the secret?"

"The secret? *Ah, God! My chest! It burns!* The secret — *the secret of the forward turrets —*"

Suddenly a film spread over Vargas's eyes. Blood flecked his lips. There was a dry rattle in his throat, and his head dropped back to the ground. His eyes were wide open, staring up into the night. He was dead.

JIMMY CHRISTOPHER UTTERED A DEEP SIGH, and rose to his feet. He was repeating reflectively: "The secret of the forward turrets! I wonder what he meant by that."

Slips McGuire said harshly, "Damn him! Why couldn't he live two minutes more!"

Tim Donovan had been watching the dying Vargas with wide-opened eyes. Now, he glanced around, and his young voice almost broke as he cried out sharply: "Jimmy! What happened to Diane? Where is she?"

Slips McGuire and Operator 5 suddenly became aware that Diane was not with them. "Why," Jimmy Christopher exclaimed, "she was here only a few minutes ago."

Slips McGuire said: "Saaay, she shouldn't have gone away. How'll we ever find her here, with all these soldiers around?"

Jimmy Christopher was bending down, examining a set of small footprints in the snow. They led at an angle toward the main highway a few hundred feet ahead. Alongside the highway there ran a railroad right-of-way, upon which the Central Empire was moving up its great guns and armored railroad cars. They could see the flares by which the Central Empire engineers were working, and they could hear the whistle of some sort of train far down the track around the bend.

Operator 5 frowned. "Those are Diane's footsteps. I wonder why she left us without saying anything."

He started out, following the footprints in the snow, with Tim Donovan and Slips McGuire behind him. They reached the railroad right-of-way, and a few feet beyond it could see the moving infantry on the road. Slips McGuire exclaimed: "Here, Jimmy, she's walked right along the railroad tracks. There's the mark of her feet on the snow."

There were several groups of Central Empire engineers along here, who paid no attention to the three of them. Had they known that the two men dressed in officers' coats and caps were the fugitives who were being sought everywhere through the night, they would have shot them without a moment's hesitation. But these engineers thought only that some high officer of the army was inspecting their works. Jimmy Christopher left Slips and Tim and approached them, asked one of the engineers in the language of the Central Empire: "Have you seen a young woman pass here within the last few minutes?"

The soldier leered. "Yes, my Colonel. Some of the men caught her examining the armored train that stopped here for a moment before going on. They have taken her around the bend, down the tracks."

Jimmy's blood raced in his veins. Diane was just reckless enough to have tried to obtain some information about the Central Empire armored trains, and to have been captured in the process. No doubt, she had thought to take a quick look and come back before Operator 5 was ready to go.

Jimmy swung away from the soldier, retraced his way to where Slips McGuire and Tim Donovan were standing about a trampled patch of snow along the right of way. Tim pointed to it.

"There's Diane's footsteps ending right here, and this seems to be all mussed up, as if there has been a fight here. Then look along there. She's walking again, but there're two pairs of big feet on either side of her."

Jimmy nodded. "She's been captured. They've taken her around the bend. Let's go.

THEY SET OFF AT A FAST PACE, and in ten minutes had reached the bend in the railroad tracks. They worked around the side of the hill, and Jimmy stopped short with a startled exclamation upon his lips.

Not fifty feet away from them was a group of Central Empire troopers, commandeered by a gaunt, moustached officer. Diane was stretched on her back across the tracks and the troopers were busy tying her down. Beyond the spot where Diane lay, perhaps three hundred feet, was one of the huge armored railroad cars employed by the Central Empire. Its headlights were fixed upon Diane, and it was slowly moving down the tracks toward them.

Slips McGuire uttered an oath. "They're going to run that train over Diane!"

Jimmy Christopher had sized up the situation in a moment. "Tim! Your knife! Get it ready!"

He moved quickly along the tracks, and without exciting suspicion approached the group who were tying Diane. One of the troopers was standing idly behind the officer, holding a sub-machine gun under the crook of his arm.

The officers glanced at Jimmy, saluted casually, and said: "You are just in time for a little amusement. We just caught this American girl, and we are going to have a little fun with her."

Diane's eyes had dilated when she saw Jimmy approach. She had been struggling before, against the bonds which the troopers were tying about her wrists and ankles. Now, she suddenly ceased struggling and her breasts began to rise and fall tumultuously as she realized that Operator 5 was going to risk everything to save her.

The officer went on speaking to Jimmy. "These American girls afford us a good deal of amusement. It's too bad we haven't some more of them here. In the East, we used to tie fifty or a hundred of them to the tracks and ride the trains over them. However, we must be satisfied with one now. You will remain for a few moments? We are ready now. Here comes the train!"

"Yes," Operator 5 said grimly. "I will remain!"

His fist came up in a merciless, smashing blow square into the face of the gaunt, Central Empire officer. The thud of that terrific blow mingled with the sound of crunching bone in the man's nose as the cartilage gave and was flattened under the impact. The man screamed and went toppling backward.

Jimmy sidestepped with swift footwork, and drove another blow to the stomach of the trooper who was holding the sub-machine gun. The man doubled over in agony, and Jimmy snatched the quick-firer out of his hand. Then he swung it toward the troopers who were tying Diane, shouted: "Move back! Move back or die!"

The troopers, astounded by the sudden command, terrified by the grim look in Jimmy's eyes as he leveled the sub-machine gun at them, leaped off the tracks to one side. A few of the other soldiers who had been watching from a little distance away began to run toward them to investigate.

Tim Donovan sprang to the track beside Diane, and slashed at the rope tying her wrists to the rails, white Slips McGuire began feverishly to do the same to the rope tying her ankles.

The huge armored train, with guns poking out at angles from either side, increased its speed and came rushing down toward them like a dreadful juggernaut of death.

The Central Empire troopers, when they understood what was taking place, uttered a savage shout and began to race toward the little group.

JIMMY CHRISTOPHER'S MOUTH TIGHTENED into a thin line and he sent a spray of lead rat-tat-tatting out of the quick-firer. He dropped a dozen of the troopers, and they stopped their rush. Now the big train was almost upon them, and Slips McGuire grasped Diane's ankles, yanked hard, and pulled her off the tracks, falling to the ground alongside. Tim Donovan leaped out of the way on the other side, and the train rumbled past. Diane had been whisked off the tracks in the nick of time.

The driver of the armored train applied screeching air-brakes, and brought it to a halt. The half-dozen men of the crew leaped from the car with rifles. They were wild at having been deprived of the pleasure of running down and crushing to death an American girl.

Jimmy Christopher wasted no time on them. There was no mercy in his heart as he sprayed them with two swift bursts of lead from the sub-machine gun. He cut them down like the wild beasts they were, and shouted to Tim who had come running around from the other side of the car: "Into that car! Get in, quick, everybody!"

Diane was on her feet now, none the worse for her experience, except that she was bruised in a dozen places. She and Slips McGuire and Tim Donovan at once grasped Jimmy Christopher's intention, and climbed hurriedly up into the cab of the electric engine. Operator 5 followed them, and thrust the machine gun at Slips McGuire. Then he swung to the controls of the cab and in a moment the huge armored train was racing up the tracks toward Ute Pass.

Rifles and machine guns barked in the night, and bullets clanged against the sides of the train. But the Central Empire had built well. They were safe behind those armored walls.

They met no effective opposition as Jimmy Christopher raced the train up the steep grade toward Ute Pass and safety.

Diane came up behind him, put a hand on his sleeve. "I — I'm sorry, Jimmy. I won't take such chances again."

"It's all right, Di," he told her gruffly. "Maybe it helped. We'd have had a tough job climbing Ute Pass without some means of transportation. Maybe it's a good thing it happened this way."

Tim Donovan was grinning like a chimpanzee. "That was fast work! We certainly picked ourselves a nice-looking train this time!"

Jimmy Christopher said soberly: "I sometimes think the good Lord must be fighting for us. He must arrange these things so that they work out. Suppose there had been a full crew on this car instead of just a half dozen men that were on it."

"Never mind," Tim said proudly. "We would have made it any-way, somehow. As you say, Jimmy, the Lord must be on our side!"

They had left the last of the Central Empire troops far behind, and ahead of them they could see the outposts of the American Defense Force on Ute Pass.

They were racing at sixty miles an hour directly toward the Americans. Jimmy sighed.

"I guess we're out of that, now. But we've got plenty ahead of us."

"You mean, about those turrets?" Diane asked soberly.

Jimmy nodded. "Those planes that flew out from Honolulu to reconnoitre the Asiatic Fleet — they never came back. Perhaps if we learn the secret of those turrets we'll know what happened to the planes."

"If Vargas had only lived to tell the rest of it!" Slips McGuire said harshly.

Jimmy, at the controls of the cab, shrugged. "We'll have to find out in some other way. But whatever happens, *we've got to discover the secret of those turrets!*"

And so, the captured troop train rumbled away, bearing these four who had gone through so much together. And for a moment the thoughts of all of them turned to what they had just left — to the shattered mountainside of Pike's Peak, to the thousands of broken, bloody bodies, and to the still, dead form of one man who had tried to betray his emperor.

CHAPTER EIGHT

The Thunderbolt

EIGHT HUNDRED MILES DUE WEST of San Francisco, a huge formation of swift bombing planes was flying in a south-south-westerly direction so as to cut across the steamship lane from Honolulu to San Francisco at about the 140th meridian.

These were the planes that had taken off earlier in the evening from San Francisco Bay. Almost an hour ago, the sun had disappeared somewhere in the east over the China Sea. Scout planes flying far out in advance of the formation as well as on either side were dropping flares upon the broad expanse of the ocean in an endeavor to locate the Central Empire Asiatic Fleet.

The men who flew these planes were a bit nervous, uncertain of themselves. These were the same men who had participated in the destruction of the Central Empire's Atlantic fleet at the Panama Canal only a short time ago. They were veteran flyers, recruited by Operator 5 from among the best men available in the country. They had faced enemy guns many times in the past, and they had no personal fear of death. Yet, there was that queer nervousness in them which has often been known to shatter the morale of a crack fighting force — a nervousness which can generally be traced to no particular source, but which has often been instrumental in changing the course of history.

In this particular case there was, perhaps, a more or less definite cause for this unquiet. That cause was the fact that all these flying fighters were aware that their leader had been deposed. They had followed Operator 5 unhesitatingly against hopeless odds in the past; and their deep confidence in him had contributed in great part to their victory at the Panama Canal. Now, however, they knew that their fate was in the hands of a board of governors without experience in military, naval, or aerial strategy.

Commander Harry Nichols, who was flying point of the leading echelon of this great air armada, was in charge of the entire formation. He was a good flyer, a brave man, and one who enjoyed the friendship and respect of his fellow flyers. But he as well as all the men under his command realized that he was no more than a good squadron commander. He was not the type — and he knew it himself — to lead such a tremendous formation into a pitched battle with a dangerous enemy.

In fact, when the Board of Governors had notified him that he was to take full charge of the attack upon the Asiatic Fleet, he had demurred. He had respectfully suggested that Operator 5 was the man more fitted for the job. But John Coburn had brusquely told him that he could either accept the job or else see one of his fellow officers placed in charge. Coburn had indicated definitely that Operator 5 would not be chosen.

So it was with reluctance that Commander Nichols had taken out the formation. And that reluctance, that knowledge of his limitations, was shared by every other pilot flying behind him.

The scouts were dropping flares.

Nichols wore a worried frown. He spoke into the inter-cockpit telephone. "Do you figure we might have missed them, Jack?"

"I don't think so, Harry," Lieutenant Tack Kerwin, his observer, told him. "We're a little too far north for the steamer lane. Hold her to this course for another twenty miles, and the way I figure it we ought to sight them."

Nichols nodded. "Send a message to San Francisco. Notify Coburn that we have not yet sighted the enemy, but expect to do so shortly. Ask if there are any further instructions."

Kerwin laughed bitterly. "Instructions! What instructions can those stuffed-shirts give us?"

NEVERTHELESS, KERWIN PROCEEDED to get in communication with the shore. Messages flashed back and forth as the immense air flotilla proceeded through the night. Finally the observer grimaced in disgust and switched to the inter-cockpit phone again. "Harry! Coburn's instructions are that we must continue to cruise until we have contacted the enemy. He says we must prevent the fleet from reaching San Francisco at all costs."

Nichols frowned. "Tell Coburn we can't stay in the air much longer. If we exceed our estimated time, we won't have enough gas left to return home."

Kerwin transmitted the message, listened for the reply, and then shut down the radio equipment with a gesture of impatience. Again he reported to Nichols, "Coburn says not to worry about the gas. He says sea planes ought to be able to land in the ocean!"

"My God!" Nichols exclaimed. He pointed downward. "Look how choppy the sea is. We'd be shattered to bits if we landed in the ocean."

Kerwin sighed. "It's too damn bad Z-7 isn't in charge here. How can we take orders from a bunch of men that don't know the first thing —"

He broke off as Commander Nichols suddenly stiffened in his seat and pointed forward to the south where one of the scout planes was dropping its flares.

There, starkly illuminated by the flare, were the leading ships of the enemy fleet!

The great, massive ships were sailing majestically eastward. The squat turrets placed well forward were plainly visible. Nichols frowned. "I wonder what those turrets are for —"

Just then his radio sputtered as the pilot of one of the scouting planes reported: "Lieutenant Miller reporting. Enemy fleet before us in full force. I see no activity on their decks, and no anti-aircraft guns are visible. They seem to be paying no attention to us. Their own planes are retiring to their mother ships. What shall I do?"

Nichols spoke swift orders into the transmitter: "All scouts will retire into the formation. Commanders of all odd-numbered squadrons will fall out of formation and increase their altitude, acting as reserve. All even-numbered squadrons form into echelon of Vs, and follow me. We will fly directly over and release our Number 1 and 2 bombs at my signal. Good luck, boys, and let's go!"

The scouts were already falling back into the formation. Half of the fighting planes — those in the odd-numbered squadrons — fell out and made up their own formation, moving swiftly northward and raising their altitude. Nichols headed his own half of the formation directly toward the enemy fleet.

The Central Empire ships appeared to be entirely undisturbed by the sudden attack from the air. They did not swerve from their course by so much as a degree, nor did they bother to douse their lights. Apparently they were deliberately making of themselves as perfect targets as they possibly could for the bombs of the American planes. The enemy planes had all left the sky and had taken refuge on the broad decks of the airplane carriers, of which there

MAR-
SHAL
KREMER

EMPEROR
RUDOLPH

BARON
FLEX-
NER

ANITA
MON-
FRED

was almost a dozen in the Asiatic Fleet.

It seemed almost unbelievable that the Emperor of the Central Empire Fleet should take absolutely no precautions to defend himself against the attack. Lieutenant Kerwin, from the cockpit behind Nichols, spoke urgently into the inter-cockpit phone: "Be careful, Harry. There's something wrong here. We may be flying into a trap."

"Can't help it, Jack. Orders are to attack as soon as we sight the enemy fleet —"

NICHOLS NEVER FINISHED THAT SENTENCE. Abruptly, without warning of any kind, both his motors began to sputter and spit; and then a sheet of flame burst from somewhere in the gas line. In a moment the plane was enveloped in fire. Flames licked at the wings on either side.

And no matter how Nicholas maneuvered his ship, he could not avoid the licking tongue of fire that reached eagerly into the cockpit. He fought the control madly, but the wings buckled, and the ship fell into a wild, uncontrolled tailspin.

Behind him, all the planes in his formation were likewise being consumed by fire.

Something strange, unexplained, dreadful, had just taken place. Four hundred powerful fighting planes of the latest design were being destroyed without an overt move from the enemy. Men died in those cockpits like rats trapped in a burning ship. The planes plummeted into the ocean with the charred, dreadfully burned bodies of the flyers still strapped in their seats.

It was such a catastrophe as had never occurred before in the history of aerial warfare. Not a single one of those eight hundred men who perished in the four hundred planes knew what had happened. They went to their death numb, startled, taken entirely by surprise. Now, the wrecked and burning planes floated on the face of the ocean like macabre beacons of death. Bits of wings and undercarriage floated away from the burning ships. And the agonized screams of men who were burning to death were drowned by the angry roar of the ocean.

Far above them, the second contingent consisting of the odd-numbered squadrons rode high in the sky, their flyers looking down with unbelieving eyes at the nightmare of death below them. They could not understand what had happened. One moment those big bombers had been flying confidently toward the enemy fleet; now, in the next instant, they were floating coffins — weird crematories for the bodies of the pilots and observers in them.

And the enemy fleet moved on steadily, majestically, never swerving from its course, riding down the burning wreckage of the planes in their path.

HIGH ABOVE THE FLEET, the remaining four hundred planes climbed even higher in a blind attempt to escape the mysterious fate that had caught their fellows. Leaderless, they knew not what to do. But for the foresight of Commander Nichols in dividing his forces, they, too, would now be nothing but burning corpses.

The commander of Squadron 1 up there, Lieutenant-Commander Lester, automatically took over control as the senior officer. He led the formation in a wide bank that headed them in a northerly direction. Lester himself was trembling as he fingered the controls of his plane. He managed to get a grip on himself, and spoke into the inter-cockpit phone to his observer: "Communicate with the Board of Governors at once. Advise them of what has happened, and ask them for further orders. They sent us into this — and still we've got to take orders from them!"

In a moment his observer informed him: "Sorry, Lester. I have just reported to Coburn, and he orders that we continue the attack. He can't understand what can possibly have happened to Nichols and the other planes. He says you are to take command of the formation."

Lieutenant-Commander Lester swore luridly. "Damn Coburn! We can't fly against something we don't understand. Imagine those governors sitting in their council room and sending us orders to go down and be burned to death. Harry Nichols and I used to be at Annapolis together. He was a year ahead of me, and I used to think he was the greatest guy in the world. Now he's cinders!"

Below them the fitful glare of the still-burning planes gave mute evidence of the danger of coming too close to the enemy fleet.

Lester's observer said shakily: "What in the Devil's name do you think could have happened to them? Did you see how they all took fire at the same time? And there wasn't even a single shot fired from that fleet!" The man shivered. "It gives me the willies!"

They were flying north-westward now, and Lester grated: "I'd like to see John Coburn and his Board of Governors down there in those burning flames."

"What are you going to do?"

"I'm going to disobey orders!" Lester barked savagely. "And I think every man in the formation will back me up. If it's mutiny, let them make the most of it!"

And so, through the night, the Asiatic Fleet of the Central Empire plowed over the ocean, across the charred corpses of Harry Nichols and his flyers, while the surviving formation of the American Air Fleet crawled back home with its tail between its legs. There was nothing now between the powerful guns of the enemy fleet and defenseless San Francisco.

CHAPTER NINE

Liberty or Death!

IN THE CAPITOL BUILDING of the city of Denver, Rudolph I, Emperor of the Central Empire, Master of Europe and Asia, Conqueror of America, held high court.

The brilliant reception room was decorated with costly hangings which covered all the wall. These hangings were the loot from American homes, institutions and museums throughout the occupied territory.

Rudolph's grey-clad storm troopers had confiscated everything of value wherever the Central Empire took possession. For American civilians in the occupied territory there was no such thing as personal property any longer. Americans from the Atlantic Coast to the Rocky Mountains, from Maine to the Mexican border, lived under the cruelest of regulations and restrictions yet devised for conquered people. Not even a man's time was his own. His home was no longer sacred. Every able-bodied man, woman and child among the civilians was compelled to perform four hours of daily labor for the conquerors. They were assigned to this work regardless of their fitness for it, regardless of their former occupation, regardless of their physical ability to perform it.

Refusal to perform this forced labor was punishable by instant death — or worse.

Vast stores of gold, silver, jewelry and other valuable possessions which had been confiscated from American citizens were stocked in warehouses of the Central Empire. Our people were reduced to a state of virtual serfdom similar to that which prevailed in Europe in the Middle Ages — except that it was far worse, for our American citizens found it difficult, if not impossible, to adapt themselves to the idea of bending the knee to a dictator.

Abortive uprisings of citizens in scattered sections were put down with ruthless cruelty. And in order to crush every possibility of resistance, mass executions were staged at frequent intervals. The headsman's axe fell with ominous frequency upon the necks of innocent and guilty alike. The merest breath of suspicion could cause a man to lose his head.

Indeed, men and women were executed even if no hint of suspicion fell upon them; for Rudolph had given to his various viceroys in charge of the conquered states the right of the high and low justice. Citizens were beheaded for the slightest infraction of the strict rules laid down by the conquerors. A disrespectful word to a Central Empire officer, the failure to stand at attention when the Central Empire flag passed, or even the whim of one in authority, was sufficient to place a man upon the scaffold.

For tonight, Rudolph had planned a little grim diversion.

IN THE HUGE COUNCIL ROOM of the Executive Mansion he sat upon a dais at the far end of the room. His thin, vicious countenance was not enhanced in appearance by the small moustache that he affected; nor did the splendid imperial robe and the crown lend him stature or dignity. Innately, Rudolph was a mean, sadistic man. This great empire over which he ruled had not been welded together by his own hands. It was his father, Maximilian I, who had risen by quick, successive steps from the position of dictator of a small European military power to the position of master of more than half the world. Maximilian had been killed during the early days of the Invasion of America, and Rudolph had ascended to the throne.

No man was more unfit to hold the destiny of millions of people in the palms of his hands. In his nature there were no such things as mercy, kindliness or friendship. He saw his great power not as a trust to be administered justly and wisely — but as a means of satisfying every craving, every passion, every lust that stirred within the depths of his unholy being.

With his accession to the supreme command of the Empire there had been inaugurated a saturnalia of humiliation, degradation, rape, torture, and death for American citizens in the occupied territory.

He sat now upon his throne, staring with glittering, greedy eyes at the five prisoners before him. These five were all gowned in long, judicial robes. Their feet were bound together at the ankles by wire which was fastened to pegs in the floor. Overhead, a series of pulleys had been suspended by posts from the ceiling, and ropes which ran down from these pulleys ended in nooses which lay loosely around the necks of the five men. The five stood silent, in stately, erect dignity. They were all well advanced in years, and their faces were well known to the American populace. They were Justices Langston, McHugh, Webber, Sabbath, and Morse of the United States Supreme Court.

They had been ferreted out and hunted down during the past few weeks by the Surveillance Department of the Central Empire. Now, they had been decked out in their judicial robes as a ghastly mockery for the occasion of their execution.

The immense room was thronged with gay officers in glittering uniforms, and with fawning courtiers who were gathered about Rudolph. Beside the Emperor's chair, one at either hand, stood Baron Flexner and Marshal Kremer — the two men to whom Rudolph owed much of his success. Flexner was the suave, wily diplomat, while Kremer was the blunt, crusty general who had led the Central Empire troops to victory all over the world.

KREMER WAS STANDING STIFF AND STRAIGHT, his bushy brows drawn together in a frown. His distaste for these proceedings was quite evident, for he was not the type of man to hide his feeling, even before the Emperor. Baron Julian Flexner, on the other hand, was bending to whisper in the Emperor's ear, a sly smile upon his face. "I regret, sire, that the Surveillance Department, was unable to hunt down the remaining two justices of the American Supreme Court. They are either dead, or they have fled across the Rocky Mountains. But I think that the ceremony will be very entertaining with these five."

Rudolph's lips twisted in a cruel smile. "It is well, Flexner. We will do the best we can. I should like to see these judges grovel before me; but the old fools do not seem afraid to die."

Flexner shrugged. "I have always found it difficult to understand these Yankee fools. They seem to love nothing but their liberty. Only a fool would be ready to die for such an abstract thing. All over the country, thousands of them have been offered their lives if they would but take the oath of fealty to you, sire. And rather than do so, they have allowed themselves to be beheaded. It is beyond my comprehension!"

Rudolph turned from Flexner and looked up at Marshal

Kremer. "What do you say, Kremer? Do you know of any way that we can make these stubborn fools acknowledge me as their rightful ruler?"

The old Marshal's face was stern, uncompromising. "I know nothing of that, sire. I am but a simple soldier. I win your battles for you, but I cannot tell you how to make men love you."

"Am I to understand," Rudolph asked silkily, "that you disapprove of my treatment of these conquered people?"

Kremer was about to answer angrily, but he restrained himself as he saw Flexner's cruel, sardonic glance fixed upon him. He said shortly: "As I told you before, your Majesty, I am only a soldier. My opinion on the problems of government means nothing. I am sure that Baron Flexner is guiding you to your satisfaction."

For a moment Rudolph gazed at Kremer as if he were inclined to probe further into the Marshal's feelings. But Flexner broke in suavely: "Marshal Kremer is a good general, sire. Let us leave him to war, which is the work he likes. Now, as to these five American judges. I have an idea —"

He bent lower and whispered in the Emperor's ear. Rudolph brightened, and nodded in approbation. "That is clever, Flexner. You are a good councillor. I shall try it at once."

He looked up and raised his voice, addressing the five prisoners. A hush suddenly descended upon the gay throng in the room as he spoke.

"You five men are about to die," the Emperor said coldly. "But —" he leaned forward, his eyes traveling swiftly from one to the other of the robed prisoners — *"there is a way by which you may preserve your lives!"*

THE FIVE JUDGES STOOD ERECT, FACING HIM, with the nooses about their necks, and their hands bound behind their backs. They said nothing, waiting for the Emperor to continue. Their bearded faces were gaunt from privation, for they had been held in solitary confinement until this moment. They were none of them men of action, having lived quiet, secluded lives in an atmosphere of learning and law. But there was a clear, fine look in their eyes, and they stood with their shoulders well back and their heads up.

Rudolph stamped his foot in impatience. "Why do you not answer me?" he demanded. "Have you lost your tongues?"

Judge Langston, who was the Chief Justice of the Supreme Court, answered for all of them. His clear, concise voice sounded without a tremor of fear.

"You have made a statement, but have asked no question that requires an answer. I will say, however, speaking for all of us, that we will do nothing to preserve our lives that may cast disgrace upon our names. We are ready to die, and we ask no favors of you!"

Rudolph's hands clenched on the arms of his chair, and his face grew white with fury. His eyes swung to the executioner who stood by the wall at a wheel to which were attached the ends of the five ropes running over the pulleys. By turning that wheel the executioner could take up the slack of the rope and proceed with the execution. The Emperor was about to utter a command to the executioner, when Flexner placed a respectful hand on his arm and whispered something.

Rudolph hesitated, then shrugged. "Very well, Flexner. See if you can do any better." Flexner said softly: "Thank you, sire." Then he straightened, and stepped down from the dais to stand facing the five condemned men. He spoke in a smooth, conciliatory voice.

"You five gentlemen are perhaps under the impression that my master, the Emperor Rudolph, is unduly severe. That is far from the truth. In conquering this country my Master is doing no more than countless other conquerors have done in the history of the world."

Flexner paused, and a wisp of a smile tugged at the corners of Justice Langston's lips.

"Are you trying," he asked, "to justify this campaign of invasion on that ground?"

Flexner shrugged. "Perhaps not to justify it, but to explain it. In the previous decade, Italy conquered Ethiopia, and made it an Italian province. That conquest was acknowledged by the League of Nations. As long as the world goes on, the mighty will subjugate the weak. My Master would be glad to show his Secret Service Operator # 5 mercy and his leniency to your countrymen if they cease resistance."

Justice Langston shook his head. "That will never be, Baron. Your Master has yet to learn that he will never be acknowledged as the rightful ruler of this country — a ruler by conquest!"

"Perhaps," Flexner said insinuatingly, "the people of America *would* recognize him, if *you* were to announce that the Supreme Court of the United States accepted him."

Rudolph, Kremer, and all those others in the room waited breathlessly for the reply. Flexner added cajolingly: "If you five members of the Supreme Court would declare for Emperor Rudolph, not only would your lives be spared, but my Master would appoint you to high places in the government of the occupied territory. You would be restored to your full previous rights and dignity, and would live honored and respected under the protection of his Imperial Majesty. In return for all this, nothing is required of you except that you acknowledge Rudolph I as the rightful ruler of America!"

THERE WAS A PREGNANT SILENCE in the room during which one might have heard a pin drop. This was Flexner's idea, which he had whispered in Rudolph's ear — to use the Supreme Court of the United States for the purpose of establishing Rudolph's right to rule over the country. The temptation which he was laying before these men was great indeed — life, position, honor — if they would but ratify the conquest. Was it within the power of a human being to withstand such temptation when he stood with the very noose about his neck?

Rudolph and all the others waited eagerly for the answer. It meant a great deal to the Central Empire, for the great mass of citizens had deep respect for the venerable members of the highest court in the land. And if they should acknowledge Rudolph, it would aid immensely in pacifying the conquered portions of the country.

Justice Langston turned sideways and looked at his associate judges. From one to the other he glanced, and no nod or word was exchanged among them. These men knew each other intimately, knew their ideals and the principles for which each stood; and no word or sign was necessary between them to convey their thoughts upon this subject. Langston's eyes met those of McHugh,

Webber, Morse and Sabbath in turn. Then the Chief Justice smiled slightly and faced Flexner once more.

He drew himself up to his full stature, and looked past Flexner at Rudolph. He spoke in the deep, resonant, imposing voice which had often been heard from the Bench of the Supreme Court: "We, a majority of the members of the Supreme Court of the United States of America, here assembled as prisoners, do hereby declare and state that you, Rudolph I, Emperor of the Central Empire, are a usurper. And we do now beg and adjure every citizen of this country to resist you by whatever means he has at hand. If the country must perish, then let it perish with honor. *Give us liberty or death!*"

There was a startled hush in the room as the echoes of Justice Langston's ringing voice rolled down from the high, vaulted ceiling. Officers and courtiers stared unbelievingly at these five men who had without hesitation spurned the chance to save their lives. And in that hush, Langston's voice came again, this time low and contained: "We are ready to die, Baron Flexner."

Now Rudolph's rage became terrible to behold. He half rose in his chair, his face suffused with a deep crimson flush of anger. His eyes were burning tintypes of hate, and his lips were twisted into a mad sneer.

"Executioner!" he shouted hoarsely. "Do your duty!"

The executioner bowed, reached over and gripped the handle of the wheel. He spun it around, and the rope tautened on the pulleys. The executioner exerted greater pressure on the wheel, and the nooses tightened about the throats of the five justices, stretching their necks painfully. With their feet fastened to the floor by the wire, the agony of the straining nooses was spread to every portion of their bodies so that every nerve became a center of excruciating pain.

"More, more!" Rudolph shouted avidly. The courtiers and the officers craned their necks to watch the torture. And Rudolph's eyes burned greedily as he strained forward so as not to miss one iota of the suffering of his victims.

Only one man of all that assemblage did not stay to see the execution finished. That man was Marshal Kremer. Quietly, he stepped back from the dais and made his way to the door. He walked swiftly through the corridor and out into the open air. Here he spat angrily in the street, and got into the staff car.

"Drive me back to headquarters," he growled at his driver. He sat silently in the car as it drove through the night, his face set in grim lines. Then, with apparent irrelevance, he said to his driver: "Some American general once said that war was Hell."

"Yes, my general," the driver replied over his shoulder, "that was the American general, Grant."

"Well," Kremer grumbled, "war may be Hell, but I thank God that I'm only a soldier — and not an emperor!"

He leaned over and spat out of the window once more.

CHAPTER TEN

Outlawed

IT TOOK THE FIVE SUPREME COURT JUDGES an hour and ten minutes to die. Justice Morse, who was the oldest and, perhaps, the feeblest of the five, went limp at the end of thirty-five minutes. Justice McHugh was the last to die — after seventy minutes of excruciating agony.

The story of the death of these heroic judges has been told many times in our history. It is needless, and it would be too gruesome, to tell that story over again here in all its harrowing details. The torture which those five brave old men endured on that day has written itself indelibly on the hearts of the nation. It has been woven into novels and plays and moving pictures. Songs have been written about Langston, McHugh, Webber, Morse, and Sabbath. Their names will live as long as America lives — nay, longer, as long as tales are told of courage and bravery and endurance.

Three times during that crucial ordeal the ropes were loosened and they were once more given a chance to accept Rudolph's terms. Each time they refused. And when the news spread by grapevine telegraph to every city and village and town and hamlet in the land, a renewed spirit of patriotism was awakened and men resolved again never to yield to the Purple Conqueror, so that those judges might not have died in vain.

But out on the West Coast, a far different set of men were meeting in the Headquarters Building of the Presidio in San Francisco.

The Board of Governors was in session again.

At the head of the long council table sat John Coburn, the Acting Governor of California, and the Chairman of the Board of Governors.

His cold glance was fixed upon Jimmy Christopher who was standing at the foot of the table and addressing the assembled governors with impassioned vigor. In a corner of the room stood Lieutenant-Commander Lester, the man who had led back the survivors of the air flotilla after the destruction of Nicholas and his men. Lester was glaring fixedly at John Coburn while Jimmy talked.

Operator 5 had both hands on the table and was leaning forward as he spoke. "Gentlemen, you have thus far made mistakes in everything that you have done. You countermanded Z-7's orders which threw our reserves into the position behind the Santa Rosa Mountains for the purpose of preventing the Central Empire divisions from driving a wedge behind our front line of defense; you ordered Commander Nichols to attack at once without testing the strength of the enemy fleet, and as a result half of our available air force has been destroyed."

His voice dropped in pitch and he spoke across the table directly at the Acting Governor of California.

"You, John Coburn, have the blood of eight hundred brave flying men on your hands. You have done us more harm since you took over command yesterday than the enemy could have done to us in a month. And now you wish to court-martial Lieutenant-Commander Lester for disobeying your orders. You wanted him to sacrifice the remaining planes because you did not think it possible that they could be destroyed in such manner. Perhaps now you are convinced that the enemy possesses a powerful secret weapon —"

Coburn arose, his hard face set in a mask of contempt. "I must remind you, Operator 5, that you are here as a subordinate for the purpose of reporting upon your activities of the last twenty-four hours. You are not here to condemn us or to defend Commander Lester. Kindly make your report now or else I shall ask you to leave the room!"

Jimmy Christopher stepped back from the table and his gaze travelled down a long line of acting governors seated in conference. He was looking for some hint of sympathy, for some suggestion that help was near.

But they were all set on preserving the dignity and the authority of their board. Men of little ability themselves, they were keenly jealous of anyone who might supplant them in the leadership of the country which they had assumed.

Jimmy bowed his head.

"Since you won't let me speak, Coburn, I shall take your suggestion and leave. I hereby notify you that I do not consider myself subject to your orders. From now on I shall conduct an independent campaign against the Central Empire!"

His ANNOUNCEMENT CAUSED a wave of excitement to sweep along the table. As he turned to go, Coburn shouted after him: "Here! You can't do that. That's mutiny. Stop. I forbid you to go!"

Jimmy Christopher did not stop. He headed grimly for the door, and Commander Lester exclaimed: "By Jove, Operator 5, I'm with you — and so is every flyer in the flotilla!"

Jimmy wrenched open the door and started out. Coburn raised his voice and yelled to the guard in the corridor: "Arrest that man!"

There was a detail of five men and a sergeant in the corridor, and as the sergeant heard Coburn's order he hesitated for a moment, then stepped forward to bar Operator 5's way.

Jimmy Christopher knew this man well.

It was Sergeant Volney, a brave soldier who had been wounded months before at the Battle of Snyder Pass. He had lost three fingers of his right hand at Snyder Pass, and upon being discharged from the hospital he had voluntarily requested an assignment to duty. Z-7 had given him this headquarters job. Volney had served as non-commissioned officer in charge of the Presidio Guard for the last month or two and he had heard with a certain degree of amazement that the Board of Governors had superseded Z-7 and Operator 5. However, it was his duty to obey those in authority, and since there had been no opposition either from the Chief of Intelligence or from Jimmy Christopher, he had assumed that everything was in order.

Now he received his first inkling that there was trouble. And it came to him in such startling fashion that the sergeant was bewildered. He was suddenly faced with the necessity of arresting the man under whom he had served with Hank Sheridan at Snyder Pass.

His face was a study of mingled emotion as he blocked Jimmy's path and said "I — I'm sorry, Operator 5. I — I've got to obey orders."

From inside the council room John Coburn's voice came to them, raised to an angry pitch: "Volney! I order you to arrest that man!"

The five privates in Volney's detail stood watching the tense scene with their rifles at rest. Commander Lester was behind

Jimmy, and close to the door of the council room.

Jimmy Christopher stood almost toe to toe with Volney. "Look here, Bob," he said tensely: "Coburn and that asinine Board of Governors will practically deliver this country hog-tied to the Central Empire if they continue the way they're going. I had a falling out with them, and if they put me behind bars it will mean stopping the plans I've made. You've got to let me through!"

The sergeant scratched his head. "If I let you through, Operator 5, Coburn will have me shot for insubordination. If I don't let you through, you'll be sore at me. I don't know what the Hell to do."

Coburn was at the door now, about to step through into the corridor, but Commander Lester swung about facing him and blocked the way.

Sergeant Volney said quickly: "Now if you were to smack me and escape —"

Jimmy's eyes flashed in swift understanding. "I get it, Bob." His fist came tip in a light jab to Volney's jaw. And miraculously, though Volney was a very heavy, stocky, powerful man, that light tap seemed to have a tremendous effect on him, for he permitted his body to sag to the floor. But even as he dropped, his left eye closed in a deliberate wink. Then he looked over at the five men of his detail, shook his head quickly in the negative, and permitted himself to collapse in a heap.

Jimmy Christopher had whirled almost in the instant of striking Volney, and now he shouted: "Into the council room, Lester!"

Commander Lester had once been a Navy half-back. He was used to signals, and quick orders, and quicker physical reactions to those orders. No sooner had Jimmy Christopher's command been uttered, than Lester launched his 190 pounds in a catapult-like lunge that sent Coburn and the others clustered in the doorway flying back into the room.

They sprawled on the floor, flung there by the force of Lester's drive, and Jimmy Christopher sprang in after him, slammed the door shut and twisted the catch.

COMMANDER LESTER PICKED HIMSELF up from the floor, grinning, and he and Operator 5, standing shoulder to shoulder, faced the assembled group of acting governors.

An automatic had appeared in Jimmy Christopher's hand, and Commander Lester drew a revolver from his hip-holster. Jimmy Christopher said coldly: "If any of you gentlemen wishes to be injured, let him make a move to stop us! Come on, Lester."

He backed up, with Lester at his side, until they reached the window. They were on the ground floor, facing east over the Presidio, towards the parade grounds.

"You first," Jimmy snapped. Lester nodded, threw a leg over the sill and vaulted to the ground outside. Jimmy was facing the angry governors.

Coburn, crouching at the head of the others, snarled: "You'll be caught, Operator 5 — caught and shot. You'll be shot for mutiny!"

Jimmy Christopher's lips were a tight, hard line. "John Coburn," he rapped, "you've done a lot of harm. You've done so much harm that I almost wonder that you haven't done it — deliberately. If I were sure of that, I'd shoot you now in cold blood. Be thankful that I'm not sure."

"You fool!" Coburn shouted. "We are the only duly constituted government of the country. If you defy us and disobey our orders you will destroy what little morale there is left!"

"I'm sorry, Coburn," Jimmy said. "I don't trust you. And I can't serve under a man I don't trust."

He turned his back on them, and sprang out of the window, joining Lester outside. For some strange reason, neither Sergeant Volney nor his detail of men had thought of running outside to intercept the fugitives at the window. Their way was clear, and they hurried across the grounds toward the Marine Hospital.

Lester followed Jimmy Christopher with a puzzled look on his face. "How the devil do you expect to escape?" he demanded. "Volney was willing to play ball with us. But the rest of the troops will obey the governors because they are the duly constituted authority. They —"

"Don't worry," Jimmy told him. "Follow me."

He led the way around to the rear of the Marine Hospital where a powerful car was waiting for them. Tim Donovan was at the wheel of the car. Jimmy Christopher smiled at Lester's look of amazement. "Yes, Commander, I ordered Tim to wait for me here. I suspected that something like this might happen. Pile in."

Lester needed no second request. Already, men were shouting behind them at the Headquarters Building. Tim Donovan moved over, and Jimmy Christopher got in under the wheel, shifted into first, and sent the car speeding away around the back of the Marine Hospital grounds toward the Park Presidio Boulevard.

Tim Donovan had refrained from asking questions, while they were starting. He had seen Jimmy Christopher and Lester come running from the direction of the Headquarters Building, and he knew that something was up. He had not bothered Jimmy with unnecessary questions. Now, however, that they were out of the Presidio grounds, he asked: "Was it a showdown, Jimmy?"

Operator 5 nodded grimly. "Just that, Tim."

Commander Lester, from the rear of the car, growled: "It's a tough break for the country, Jimmy. It means we will have civil war at a time when we can't afford to be divided. But it's the only thing that we can do. If we left the direction of the country in the hands of that Board of Governors for another forty-eight hours, it would be all over —"

He stopped short as Jimmy Christopher stepped down sharp on the brakes.

From the direction of Golden Gate Park, directly ahead of them, a big U.S. Army truck was racing straight toward them. Looking through the rear window, Lester could see a close-packed group of cars coming after them out of the Presidio grounds. Coburn must have acted fast. He must have sent a radio alarm to the military guards in Golden Gate Park to head them off. Now their retreat was cut off as well.

LESTER'S FACE DARKENED WITH ANGER. His gun leaped into his hand. "Dammit, we'll fight it out —"

"Hold everything," Jimmy Christopher called back to him. "We're not caught yet. He started the car again and made a sharp left turn into Cabrillo Street, and headed east toward the Bay. Behind them, on the boulevard, shots began to crash, as the Army trucks, then the pursuing cars from the Presidio, swung into Cabrillo Street after them.

Many of those men on the trucks and in the cars knew Jimmy Christopher personally, and also knew Commander Lester. But they were blindly obeying the orders of the men who had assumed the leadership of the country. To their minds, Operator 5's action in defying the orders of the Board of Governors was the action of a bitter man disappointed at having had the supreme command taken from him.

They had had no chance to observe closely the result of the suicidal strategy of the governors. Reports of the progress of the war for the last two days had been kept from the public. Lester had not been permitted to make public his report of the destruction of the air flotilla. Neither had the news been given out of the swift advance of the Central Empire troops in Southern California.

Therefore, those pursuing soldiers assumed that Operator 5 had defied the governors out of personal ambition.

Jimmy Christopher, driving skillfully eastward toward the Bay, went over the situation swiftly in his mind. There would, of course, be hundreds of men — like Sergeant Volney, for instance — who would continue in their solid faith in Operator 5. But there were many more thousands who would not know how to judge between both sides, who would think that Coburn and his council were in the right. As Lester had pointed out, if Jimmy Christopher were to attempt to enlist the sympathies of the great masses of people, the country would inevitably split into two armed camps, would engage in civil war and thus give the Central Empire an opportunity to complete its conquest.

He realized that he should have thought of all this before throwing down his challenge to Coburn. But even if he *had* thought of it, he reflected bitterly, it would have been impossible for him to remain under the orders of that grossly incompetent body of men. They had refused to listen to reason, refused to follow the advice of a seasoned campaigner like Z-7. And the only course of action open to Operator 5 was that which he had taken. Now he was being hunted.

Tim Donovan, sitting beside him, put a hand on his knee. "Keep a stiff upper lip, Jimmy. I know what you're thinking. You're thinking it might even be better to knuckle under to Coburn and those others. Well, don't you do it. You do as you think right. I've never known you to be wrong before, Jimmy."

The lad's faith and devotion touched Jimmy. But he didn't reply.

He was sparing his breath. He was pushing the car for all it was worth, while the army truck and the pursuing autos sent volley after volley after them. Jimmy was gaining on them slightly. He swung south, then east again along Fulton Street. He gained a block on the pursuers at Alamo Square, and Lester and Tim were just beginning to think that they might get away.

Then disaster struck. For ahead of them, at the east corner of Alamo Square, another army truck swung into Fulton Street, blocking their way.

Jimmy Christopher stepped on the brake hard, to avoid a head-on collision. Lester and Tim were thrown violently forward in their seats. Lester swore, and snatched out his gun.

"Well," he rapped out, "I guess it's all up. We'll make those guys eat lead before they get us!"

JIMMY CHRISTOPHER TWISTED AROUND in the seat and gripped his wrist. "No, Lester. These boys are all Americans. They're doing what they think is right, obeying orders. To them we're nothing but mutineers. We can't shoot them down."

Lester lowered his eyes. "But to be trapped like this! They'll throw us in jail and we'll rot there while the Central Empire walks over the country."

Men from the truck ahead as well as from the cars behind were hurrying toward them.

Tim Donovan looked up at Operator 5, and the boy's eyes were misty. "Gee, Jimmy, after all you've done for the country, it's a damn shame that you should be thrown into jail." Suddenly tears were flowing openly from the lad's eyes.

Jimmy Christopher shrugged. "It's all in the game, kid. You've got to learn to take it on the chin."

He opened the door, and stepped out to meet the approaching soldiers. As far as he was concerned, it was the end. He had done his best, and he thought bitterly that his best had not been good enough this time. He was sorry now that he had permitted Slips McGuire to take him away from the battle at the Salton Sea the previous day.

It would have been far better, he reflected, if he had been killed with Cahill and those others back there on the El Centro road.

He threw back his shoulders and waited while his prospective captors surrounded him.

Commander Lester and Tim Donovan got out of the car also, and ranged themselves shoulder to shoulder with him. The pursuing soldiers came up to them from both directions, and in a moment they were faced with a semi-circle of glittering bayonets.

This time, significantly, Sergeant Volney was not here. The officer in charge was an infantry captain named Francis Coburn. He was a nephew of John Coburn, and had only that day been transferred from field duty to staff work with the Board of Governors. He was a young, priggish dandy, with a little waxed moustache which he kept carefully trimmed. He now snapped at Jimmy, "Operator 5, you are under arrest by order of the Board of Governors!"

Jimmy Christopher bowed with courteous irony. "Very well, Captain, make your arrest. It seems that the Coburn family is having things all its own way."

Coburn said brusquely: "We'll take Lester and this boy with us, too."

Jimmy Christopher's eyes narrowed. "There's no need for that, Captain. Commander Lester and Tim Donovan, I am sure, were not included in your order."

Coburn smirked. "You are mistaken, Operator 5, about Commander Lester. My uncle expressly ordered me to place him under arrest as well, on two charges — first, for failing to obey orders and refusing to attack the enemy fleet; second, for aiding and abetting you in your escape just now."

Lester shrugged. "If Operator 5 is going to be in jail, I might as well be in jail, too. But why the boy? What has Tim Donovan done?"

Captain Coburn said stiffly: "The Board of Governors orders that all those who have been associated with Operator 5 are to be placed under arrest. That includes Tim Donovan here, Miss Elliot, and Slips McGuire. Also, Sergeant MacTavish and Operator 5's sister, Nan. We are going to make sure that no one who is loyal to Operator 5 remains at liberty to foment rebellion against the Board of Governors!"

JIMMY CHRISTOPHER'S BLOOD BOILED. Upon returning from Pike's Peak, he had left Diane and Slips McGuire at the Custom House near the waterfront. His sister, Nan, and the Canadian Sergeant, MacTavish, were in San Diego at the time, There was no way of warning them of the impending arrest.

Tim Donovan knew what Operator 5 was thinking, and the boy's eyes wore a desperate, harassed look. It seemed to be the end.

Captain Coburn, with his lips twisted into a sneering smile, moved aside so that Lester, Jimmy and Tim could step between the two files of the arresting squad of soldiers.

And just then, a strange, whining noise suddenly began to intrude itself upon their ears. At first it was low, ominous, coming somewhere from the west. Jimmy Christopher stopped short, and turned his gaze toward the ocean. The whining sound grew louder by the second, rose in volume until its shrill crescendo tore at their eardrums with overpowering force. The dreadful noise seemed to fill all the air about them.

Operator 5 shouted: "It's a shell! Dive for cover, everybody!" He shoved Tim and Lester ahead of him, fairly thrust them to the ground, and threw himself beside them. A few of the soldiers in the arresting detail were experienced veterans of the World War. They, too, recognized that terrifying whining sound and threw themselves to the ground.

Captain Coburn and some of the younger men stood there dazed, frightened by the noise. Though Coburn had served at the front in the present invasion, he had been stationed, at the instance of his uncle, in a quiet sector up near the Canadian border where there was little activity. This was the first time he had heard the distinctive sounds made by one of the enemy's huge shells.

It was all over in a space of moments. The whine of the shell changed to a screech, and was followed by a terrific explosion that shook the ground under their feet. Jimmy Christopher leaped to his feet and gazed westward toward a fume of smoke less than a dozen blocks away. He pointed excitedly. "That's where the shell struck. Right square on the City Hall building!"

Young Captain Coburn was stuttering, "What — where — what

is it?"

Tim Donovan grinned at him. "That, my brave Captain, is an enemy shell. The Central Empire Fleet is bombarding San Francisco!"

Almost on the heels of Tim's statement, that whining sound was repeated, but this time it came in multiples.

CHAPTER ELEVEN

The Gamble

ALL THOUGHT OF ARRESTING OPERATOR 5 had fled from Coburn's mind. His face grew suddenly white and pasty. That tremendous metallic whine caused a din in the air that was enough to frighten any man who heard it for the first time, Now, all over the city, shells were bursting. Coburn was cowering, and a shiver ran through his frame at each new explosion.

Jimmy looked at him pityingly. "You'd better get some place and hurry up, Coburn."

The young captain turned and staggered away, regardless of the open contempt of the soldiers under him. Many of these started to melt away down the side streets as they saw their captain departing.

Tim Donovan suddenly began to laugh. "That's a new one on us, Jimmy — being saved from arrest by the enemy!"

Lester was more serious. "Those are eighteen-inch guns, Operator 5," he said.

He had to raise his voice now to be heard above the fury of sound. All about them panic-stricken women — those who had not yet taken refuge across the Bay — were rushing out of their homes, terrified lest the next shell should strike close to them.

Jimmy Christopher said soberly, "Eighteen-inch guns, Lester. You know what that means? It means that their ships must be standing out about thirty miles to sea. We haven't a gun here in Frisco that could reach them. They can bombard the city off the map, and we can't touch them."

Nobody opposed them as they got back into the car. Jimmy drove around the Army truck which had been left standing in the middle of the street, and sent the car speeding eastward toward the Bay front.

Lester bent forward in the rear seat and shouted to Jimmy above the din of the bombardment: "The planes — how about my taking the planes up and seeing what I can do —"

Jimmy Christopher shook his head. "You know what happened to Nichols? The same thing would happen to you."

"Okay. I'll signal you within an hour, We can't send the planes against that the fleet until we learn what their secret is."

Jimmy had to make a detour twice in order to avoid deep chasms in the street which had been caused by striking shells. The city was being rocked by thunderous explosions coming in swift succession. Tall buildings were crumbling under the bombardment, and the rumbling of the falling structures added a deep, menacing undertone to the shrill whining and the sharp detonations of the shells.

Tim Donovan, beside Operator 5, asked: "But how can we discover the secret, Jimmy? All you learned from Vargas was that it had something to do with turrets —"

They had reached the Custom House now, and they got out of the car, and ran toward the building. To the north they could see tall flames licking up to the sky from Telegraph Hill. Shells were dropping there in a steady, continuous barrage. As yet, the buildings close to the waterfront had not been struck. At any moment now, however, the barrage might move slightly to the east and to the south, and fall upon the four hundred planes of Lester's command who were riding in the Bay.

Jimmy Christopher snapped to Lester, "Get over to the Bay, Commander. Take your planes up. Get them out of danger."

"But where'll I take them, Operator 5?"

"Fly across to Richardson Bay. They're not shelling over there. Hold your planes in readiness for a signal from me. Are they all fueled up?"

Lester nodded. "All gassed and serviced, and ready to go."

"Okay. I'll signal you within an hour, using the F Code."

Lester's eyes were sparkling at the prospect of some sort of action. "Wait till the boys hear that you've taken charge of the flotilla again!"

Tim Donovan chirped: "Suppose Coburn and his monkeys try to give orders?"

Commander Lester grinned. "Just let them try!"

HE STARTED AWAY, AND JIMMY CALLED after him, "Leave me two planes with a pilot in each, Lester. I may need them."

Operator 5 and Tim hurried into the Custom House building, and found Z-7, Diane and Slips McGuire waiting for them. Z-7 was pacing the floor in impotent impatience. When he saw Jimmy he rushed over to him. "Jim, I can't stand this inactivity! They're shelling the city, and there's nothing I can do. And those governors are probably sitting around and waiting for an inspiration!"

Jimmy Christopher demanded quickly, "Did you arrange for the freighter that I asked you about?"

Z-7 nodded. "There's a ten-thousand-ton Mexican ship tied up in Tennessee Cove, across the mountains from Sausalito. I got eight hundred men out of the city across the ferry in gangs of twenty-five and fifty at a time. They're on board the ship now, but I wasn't able to get them all weapons. There are about a hundred sub-machine guns, two hundred rifles, and four crates of grenades. Outside of that they had to bring their own arms. They're a lot of antiquated rifles that we found in the warehouse. They've been condemned by the War Department, and were never thrown out. Some of the men are equipped with those. Then there are a few farmers from the back country who brought scythes.

"It's not much of a crew if you've got anything ticklish in mind, but there's plenty of spirit among them!"

"They'll do," Operator 5 said grimly. He swung on Diane and Slips. "I've got two planes out on the Bay. You and Slips and Tim will take one of them and fly to San Diego. Contact Nan and MacTavish, and wait for word from me. Z-7, you and I are flying to Tennessee Cove."

Tim Donovan plucked at Jimmy's sleeve. "Hey, Jimmy! I'm sticking with you and Z-7. I smell a lot of action coming!"

Suddenly, the din of the whining shells and the rumbling explosions ceased with startling abruptness. They all dashed out.

"The fleet has stopped shelling us!" Z-7 exclaimed.

Jimmy nodded. "They're probably going to send a demand for our surrender. They may give us three or four hours to answer. Now is the time for us to act. Hurry! We've got to make this snappy!"

They left the car in front of the Custom House and ran the few blocks to the waterfront. As they approached, they saw the majestic sight of Lester's four hundred seaplanes rising into the air to fly north toward Richardson Bay.

They watched while the planes took off, squadron by squadron, flying low over Yerba Buena Island. In a short time, the Bay was clear of planes except for the two which Jimmy Christopher had ordered.

They found a small abandoned outboard motorboat tied up at a pier, and piled into it.

As Operator 5 sent the motorboat scurrying across the Bay toward the two planes still floating there, Slips McGuire pointed a shaking finger north. "Jimmy! Look at that!"

A single shell from the enemy barrage had struck the Oakland Bridge. Though the strong structure had not been entirely destroyed, there was a great gap in the bridge of perhaps a hundred feet, and the twisted, torn girders hung from each end of the gap. In the Bay there floated bits of the metal and of human bodies. Men and women had been caught in the act of fleeing across that bridge when the shell struck.

JIMMY CHRISTOPHER TURNED HIS EYES away from that ghastly sight. He brought the motorboat up alongside the first of the two planes, and helped Diane and Slips into it. The pilot nodded to him, and Jimmy ordered: "Head straight for San Diego."

He waved goodbye to them, then set the boat in motion again and pulled up alongside the second of the two planes. He and Z-7 and Slips got into this one, and in a moment the two planes had taken off.

Ten minutes later Jimmy's plane came down to a smooth landing in Tennessee Cove, alongside a tall, black-hulled Mexican freighter on whose prow appeared the name: *San Isidro*.

Jimmy, Tim Donovan and Z-7 climbed up to the deck of the freighter, and Jimmy called down to the pilot of the plane: "You can take off again and fly across to Richardson Bay. Join Commander Lester and the flotilla there, and tell him he'll hear from me in the next couple of hours."

The decks of the freighter were alive with men — men in assorted uniforms of the various branches of the American Defense Force, as well as men in civilian clothes.

The three new arrivals ascended to the bridge, and shook hands with Captain Yarman, commanding the *San Isidro*. Yarman was not a member of the Navy, but he was a stocky, weatherbeaten sailor. His closely-cropped grey hair, his seamed leathery countenance, gave no hint as to his age. He might have been forty or sixty. But Operator 5 knew that this man had sailed the Seven Seas even before the days of steam.

Yarman said: "Well, Operator 5, everything is ship-shape. The Mexican crew was glad to turn the ship over to us. We're ready to sail at a moment's notice. And those six hundred men of yours, Z-7, are rarin' to go." He painted down toward the decks. "Listen to 'em yelling for action!"

Jimmy Christopher nodded, and stepped to the rail of the bridge. The men below were talking and shouting excitedly, lining the rails below, speculating among themselves as to what the mission was for which they had been asked to volunteer. Now, when they saw Operator 5 at the bridge, they all stopped talking and turned to face him expectantly.

JIMMY CHRISTOPHER RAISED HIS VOICE so that it carried across the length of the deck to the men massed below him.

"You've all been asked to volunteer on a blind mission. It speaks well for the spirit of the country that Z-7 was able to get together six hundred men who were willing to risk their lives blindly. But before I go any further, there is something I've got to tell you. The Board of Governors under John Coburn has relieved Z-7 and myself of all command. In fact, they have ordered my arrest. I just escaped from a detail that was sent to take me in custody. So, if you follow me on this mission, you will be following a man without standing, who is wanted for court-martial, and you may all make yourselves liable to the same punishment."

He paused for a moment, and one of the men down below on the deck shouted, "To Hell with that, Operator 5. To Hell with the Board of Governors. We're with you!"

That shout was taken up from throat to throat, until six hundred stentorian voices were shouting the willingness of their owners to follow Operator 5. Jimmy Christopher's eyes glowed warmly. These were the men who formed the rank and file of America. They knew him, knew the things he had done in the service of his country. They had faith and confidence in him; and that faith and confidence at this time gave Jimmy Christopher the spur that he needed to go on with his plans. He waited until the shouting died down, raising his hand for silence. Then he went on with a slight catch in his voice.

"I'm going to do everything that a man could possibly do to justify your trust in me. The thing that we're going to do tonight is the thing that I regard as imperative. Our chances of success are about three out of ten. In the event of failure, we will none of us survive. If we succeed we may save San Francisco from destruction and halt the Central Empire advance; if we fail we will be disgraced in death, and no one will have any sympathy for us. With that in mind, are you still willing to go on?"

The shouts of acquiescence that came up from the decks left no doubt in Jimmy's mind as to how these men felt. He drew a deep breath, and continued, explaining his plan.

"Although the Board of Governors has tried to keep the news from becoming public, you may know that half of our air flotilla was destroyed by the enemy fleet without firing a shot. I have definite information that the enemy's ships are equipped with mysterious turrets, and I think that there is some machinery in those turrets which caused the destruction of our planes, and the loss of the lives of eight hundred pilots. It is my purpose, men, to discover the secret of those turrets. In order to do so, we are going to steam out of here in this old ship, *and try to capture a Central Empire battleship!*"

A gasp of amazement at the very daring of this seemingly impossible plan went up from the six hundred men on the deck. Jimmy remained silent as the idea took root among them. Then, as they grasped the significance of the thing that they were going to do, a low cheer came up from them. They understood now why he had told them that their chances of success were only three in ten. And yet they were willing and eager to go ahead.

"We're with you, Operator 5!" a shout went up. "We'll follow you all the way."

Jimmy Christopher suddenly smiled. He swung on Captain Yarman. "Get under way, Captain! I think we're going to make history tonight!"

CHAPTER TWELVE

Men Without a Country

THIRTY MILES OFF THE COAST of California, near the Farallon Islands, the mighty Asiatic Fleet of the Central Empire was drawn up in battle array. The great ships rocked gently in the ocean's swell, riding broadside on toward the invisible coast of America. The long wicked tubes of steel which were the immense eighteen-inch guns of the Asiatic Fleet were poking their snouts up into the sky.

It was from here that the fleet had conducted the initial bombardment of San Francisco. These guns, the greatest ever mounted on a battleship, had sent their tremendous projectiles of destruction hurtling through the air at incredible speed to give the City a taste of what would follow when the bombardment began in earnest. Now those guns were silent, for a plane had taken off for San Francisco, bearing an emissary with a demand for immediate, unconditional surrender.

Four hours' grace was to be given the city; then the shelling would be resumed. And Admiral Baroda had instructed his emissary to notify the Board of Governors that if they refused to surrender, not one stone would be left standing upon another in San Francisco or in the other Bay cities.

Baroda had cunningly chosen this spot from which to conduct the bombardment, as it gave him a supply base on the Farallon Islands. Now, he sat in the sumptuously equipped cabin on board the flagship, *Koenig*. His squadron commanders were grouped in a semi-circle about his desk. Messengers from the telegraph room came in at intervals with reports from the various units of the fleet, giving their position. The messengers also brought reports from the scout cruisers which were thrown out in a far-flung line in either direction from the main body of the fleet.

Baroda was giving orders to his senior officer in charge of the aircraft carriers. "It will not be necessary, Von Goltz, to prepare our planes to take off again. I believe that the Americans will surrender after the taste of bombardment which we have already given them. However —" he shrugged and smiled meaningly — "if they should refuse to surrender, we can always get the planes ready. How long would it take you?"

Von Goltz spread his hands. "I could have them up at an hour's notice, my Admiral. My men are anxious to drop a few souvenirs along the coast. If you would but give me permission —"

"No, no. There is still half of the American flotilla which we did not destroy. I wish to have the air entirely clear of our own fliers in case the Americans should be foolish enough to try to attack us again. You will not permit any of our own planes to go up unless I give the word."

Von Goltz smiled. "As you wish, my Admiral."

Baroda looked out through the window of his cabin, from which he could see the foredeck of the *Koenig,* as well as the decks of a dozen other ships. On each ship a long gibbet had been erected, and from each of these gruesome scaffolds there swung the bodies of a dozen of the American prisoners who had been hanged that morning. There were men and women among these victims, their dead bodies swinging piteously with the swinging of the ship.

Baroda chuckled. "We will keep those corpses hanging on the decks. Even if they begin to smell a little it will be worth keeping them there for the Americans to see when we steam into San Francisco Bay. The fools expect mercy if they surrender. They will get it — with a hempen rope!"

Baroda turned back from the window to glance at his aides.

"Gentlemen," he said, "after San Francisco we will take Los Angeles and San Diego. Then we sail down the coast of Mexico. In one month, my friends, we shall be the masters of the Pacific Ocean; then to Australia. And in sixty days there will be no continent on the face of the earth over which the flag of our Master, Emperor Rudolph I, does not fly!"

The men in the cabin shouted as with one voice: "Hail, Rudolph!" And the cabin resounded with their praise of the Master, while the pitiful corpses of the executed Americans swayed limply on the gibbets outside. And while these men were celebrating their expected victory, the black hull of a tramp steamer was drifting out to sea in the direction of the fleet. The first hint of its presence came when the lookout in the crow's nest of the Central Empire cruiser *Mongol* sighted its unwieldy shape.

THE *MONGOL* WAS THE NORTHERNMOST scout cruiser of the Asiatic Fleet. It had cruised far to the north that afternoon, in search of any stray American shipping which it might capture. It was now returning to join the rest of the fleet at the Farallon Islands.

Captain Von Kunst, the commander of the *Mongol,* hurried out on deck to see the ship which the lookout had sighted.

He snatched the glass from his junior officer, focused it on the dark, unwieldy-looking freighter.

His eyes swept the deck, and then the bridge.

There was no sign of life on the decks, and nothing on the bridge.

It carried no flag, but a slight trickle of smoke was coming from its stacks.

Von Kunst frowned. "It would appear to be a derelict," he told his junior officer. "But her boilers are working. There is something queer about that ship. Fire a gun across her bows. There must be someone aboard her if she has steam on."

The mate saluted, and stepped to the gunners' telegraph. He issued swift orders, and in a moment one of the forward guns of the *Mongol* belched smoke and flame in a thunderous explosion. The shot passed squarely athwart the bow of the derelict ship. Von Kunst watched closely, but the ship did not seem to swerve at all in her aimless course. Though she had steam on, she seemed to be drifting without direction. He focused his glass on the prow, in an effort to discern her name. After straining his eyes he made it out; *San Isidro.*

He growled: "It is a Mexican ship. Perhaps it was sent adrift in the panic when our fleet bombarded San Francisco."

"Shall we board her, sir?" his mate asked.

"Why not? It may have arms, or even gold. These Mexicans are, no doubt, running arms and ammunition to the Americans. Get ready the cutter. We will send an ensign aboard her."

The *Mongol's* course was changed slightly so as to bring her across the bows of the drifting derelict. When they were within a hundred yards of her, an ensign was ordered to lower the cutter and go over to investigate. Von Kunst still kept his glass fixed on the *San Isidro,* studying it carefully, seeking some sign of life. But there was none.

Operator #5

He focused his glass on the windows of the chart room behind the bridge. Then he bent forward, peering closely. "I think I see a man at the wheel. There is something strange about this —"

Suddenly he made up his mind. "Recall the cutter!" he ordered. "I suspect something. Order all crews to battle stations. This may be a ruse of the damned Yankees!"

The cutter was put up on the davit once more, and a bugle shrilled the call to battle stations. Now the two ships were within hailing distance of each other, and the quartermaster of the *Mongol* was twisting the wheel in an effort to avoid a collision. The crews took their battle stations, and the long guns were rapidly trained upon the *San Isidro.*

Von Kunst said to his mate: "Perhaps I am a fool, but it is better to be on the safe side. That ship may be drifting aimlessly toward us, but then again I was almost sure that I saw a man at the wheel before. Now I do not see him."

"I think, sir," his mate told him, looking through another glass, "that I can see where the wheel is lashed. *There, look!* By God, it *is* a trick!"

THE MATE WAS POINTING EXCITEDLY at the *San Isidro.* For suddenly, now that only a bare hundred feet separated the two ships, the decks of the freighter suddenly became alive with swarming men. They clustered at the rail, some holding planks, some ropes, ready to grapple the huge cruiser to their small freighter. Von Kunst's face purpled as he saw a small group appear from the chart room of the *San Isidro,* on the bridge.

The derelict freighter had suddenly become a lively enemy!

Von Kunst's lips twisted in a sneer. "What fool's business is this!" he snapped. "The fools are mad. They but commit suicide!"

He leaped to the gun telegraph, seized the speaking tube, and barked into it in rapid succession the following orders: "Batteries prepare to fire! Battery A, fire! Battery B, fire! Battery C, fire! Battery D, fire!

The huge ship rumbled as his orders were obeyed. One after the other the four batteries on the port side of the *Mongol* belched their load of destruction. The battery commanders had hastily set the guns to strike below the *San Isidro*'s waterline. And as each gun in turn spoke its sharp report, the old freighter shivered from stem to stern. Water rushed in through the cruel wounds in her side, and she began to list to starboard. Suddenly a man at the halyard of the *San Isidro* pulled at a rope and the Stars and Stripes began to rise above the freighter.

All those men on board her, waiting with antiquated rifles, with scythes, with whatever weapons they had been able to gather, burst into the swinging melody of the "Star Spangled Banner." And as the inspiring tones of that song rose in competition with the vicious booming of the *Mongol's* cannon, the men at the rail threw their ropes and grappled the freighter to the high deck of the Central Empire cruiser. With their own ship sinking, their bridges were burned behind them. They had to conquer or die!

Now the men of the *Mongol* began to pour a withering fire into the Americans on the decks of the lower ship. Dozens fell, but others rushed to replace them, laid planks from one deck to the other and began to run up them. From every point of vantage on the freighter, Americans began to answer the Central Empire fire with the few machine guns in their possession.

Jimmy Christopher raced down from the bridge, to lead the first wave of the attack.

Now the *San Isidro* was sinking fast, supported only by the grappling ropes which had been thrown by the American crew onto the Purple ship. Men were dropping all about as the spiteful bark of rifles and the staccato rat-tat-tat of machine guns filled the air.

The first wave of the American attack was checked by the deadly fire of the Purple crew. But now, with the Americans responding to their fire, the second wave pushed across the planks. A dozen men, with Jimmy Christopher in the lead, reached the deck of the Central Empire ship. At once they were surrounded, outnumbered by the Purple seamen.

But other Americans were swarming aboard, faster and faster now. Tim Donovan with Z-7 and Captain Yarman had also left the bridge and they were now pushing across the planks to the enemy decks. It was but a matter of minutes before there was not a single living American left aboard the *San Isidro*. They had carried the battle to the enemy.

Operator #5

THE CREW OF THE *MONGOL* put up a stubborn resistance. But these men were themselves recruited from conquered nations in the Orient. They were fighting for their Master whom they did not know and whom most of them had never even seen, while the Americans were urged onward by the very desperation of their cause.

They knew that behind them lay a sinking ship. Defeat meant death, and disgrace. Victory meant everything. So they fought recklessly, not counting the odds. And they surged forward irresistibly while the decks of the *Mongol* grew red and slippery with the blood of dead and dying men.

The odds were almost two to one, but the element of surprise as well as the element of desperation lay with the Americans. Each group fought its way toward a definite section of the ship, in accordance with prearranged instructions issued by Operator 5. They were not fighting aimlessly. For each group was endeavoring to seize a key position on the ship.

The group under Z-7 lost half its men, but successfully fought its way down into the engine room. Jimmy Christopher, at the head of his group, stormed the bridge. And once the bridge was taken the battle was as good as won.

The hideous emblem of the crossed broadswords and the severed head was lowered from the flagstaff, and the Stars and Stripes took its place. Of the six hundred original members of that boarding party, one hundred and fifty-seven were alive at the end of the forty minutes.

Of that hundred and fifty-seven, fewer than thirty were entirely without wounds. The cost of the victory had been dreadful in its toll of lives. But the results were beyond belief.

Once the ship was theirs, it took the Americans more than an hour to secure the prisoners, clear the decks of the dead, and move the wounded to places of comfort where they could be treated. Z-7, who had received a bullet wound in the groin, managed to whisper through pallid lips, "We've done it, Jimmy! Have you got the secret of the turrets?"

Operator 5 pressed his hand. "I'll get it now. I had to find you first." He gave orders to have the wounded Intelligence Chief carried upstairs for medical treatment, and waited until he had seen

him on the way. Then Operator 5 went up on deck again, where Tim Donovan was waiting for him.

HE LED THE WAY FORWARD to where a squat turret-like structure reared out from the deck to a height of perhaps five feet. There was a small trap-door in the top of the turret, and there were six apertures at equal intervals in the round wall of the structure. One of the Americans was waiting there with a set of keys which he had taken from the Central Empire Supply Quartermaster. Jimmy took the keys and tried one after the other until he found one which opened the trap door. He lifted it up, and peered inside.

A queer machine met his gaze. There were two small motors, connected with a reservoir, the glass top of which showed an amber-colored liquid. Between the reservoir and the motors there was an oblong metal box some two feet in length and one foot wide. From this box six tubes ran to the fixed apertures in the wall. All of the machinery was clean-looking, well-kept, and covered with black japanning.

Tim Donovan waited for perhaps ten minutes while Jimmy Christopher poked around inside. At last Jimmy Christopher stuck his head up through the trap-door. There was a look of subdued triumph in his eyes.

"Tim!" he exclaimed. "Hurry to the wireless room. Send the signal to Commander Lester. Use the F Code. Tell him to take off at once to attack the Central Empire Fleet. Give him the location — off the Farallon Islands!"

Tim stared at him. "The turrets, Jimmy —"

Operator 5 hugged the lad to him. "I've fixed it, Tim, I've fixed it! They were using an infra-red ray which is capable of piercing the covering of the gas line of a plane, and igniting the gasoline mixture. They've got one of these turrets on every ship. When the flotilla under Nichols approached, they merely released the infra-red rays, and the planes burst into flame. Lester's half of the flotilla escaped because they had risen so high that the infra-red rays did not reach them. Had they decreased their altitude they, too, would have been destroyed."

"But how about the turrets now, Jimmy? Won't they be able to release the infra-red rays again —"

"I've been working on this machine, Tim. I increased the frequency of the rays by a third. We'll take down the American flag and move over into position alongside the enemy fleet. When Lester arrives, I'll release our stepped-up infra-red rays at the frequency at which I have set the rays on this ship, they should cut across the sky in such a way as to intercept the rays from the other ship, which will meet our own rays at an angle of exactly twenty-two and a half degrees. At that angle the rays of the fleet will be absorbed by our own increased frequency rays. If my theory is right, there will be no danger to planes flying at the fleet from a direction directly over us. You will tell Lester that, Tim. Now, hurry."

Tim hesitated. "What if your theory is wrong, Jimmy?"

Operator 5 shrugged. "You can tell Lester that it's only my theory. If he wants to take the chance, let him come."

WHILE CAPTAIN YARMAN moved the *Mongol* into a position between the Asiatic Fleet and the coastline, Jimmy Christopher waited tautly on the bridge. He was watching carefully for any undue activity among the Central Empire ships.

Tim Donovan, who had been in the radio room, came running excitedly across the bridge.

"Jimmy!" the lad exclaimed. "I've just intercepted a message from the Board of Governors to the American Defense Force in the front lines. Coburn has given his answer to the emissary from the Asiatic Fleet. They are going to surrender unconditionally. They have ordered the American Defense Force to cease fighting. They say they are surrendering in order to avoid destruction of the entire coastline!"

Operator 5's eyes flashed angrily. "I knew they'd do that. I was hoping we could beat them to it."

Captain Yarman had some out of the chart room, and he had heard Jimmy's announcement. Now he approached Jimmy Christopher. "They surrendered?" he asked.

Jimmy nodded. "You realize where that leaves us, Captain. We're men without a country. Well be attacking a nation with whom our own country has made peace."

"To Hell with that!" Yarman said. "I hope you're going through with it anyway!"

"Yes, Captain, we're going through with it. Even if the Board of Governors surrenders a hundred times, there will be plenty of men in the country who will still want to fight."

Suddenly, the low, distant drone of many airplane motors came to their ears. They looked up into the sky toward the east.

"There they are!" Tim Donovan exclaimed excitedly. "I told Lester to fly straight over our ship, and spread over the fleet. I told him it was taking a chance. I told him you didn't know whether your theory was right or wrong. And he said he'd take a chance on Operator 5."

Captain Yarman said: "Don't you want to get into the wireless room and send him orders?"

"No," Jimmy told him. "I've done my part. From here on it's Lester's show."

They watched breathlessly while the great flotilla passed high over their heads, the concentrated droning of their motors making music to the ears of the men on the *Mongol.*

Lester's machine, in the lead, passed overhead without accident. Squadron after squadron of the other planes followed him. Nothing happened. No flames burst from their fuel tanks.

Jimmy's face was beaded with perspiration. He had won! The enemy's rays were completely counteracted by the rays from the *Mongol.*

Tim Donovan shouted: "They're through! They've come through!"

And now, the enemy fleet was stirring.

Upon the approach of the American planes, they had set their turrets, fully expecting that the reckless Americans would go crashing into the ocean in flames in a repetition of the previous performance.

But now that the big bombers were overhead, sudden panic spread through the Central Empire Fleet.

It was too late for them to do anything.

Relying entirely upon those turrets, they had not equipped the ship with anti-aircraft guns.

Lester's squadrons spread overhead above that fleet like aveng-

ing angels. Bombs hurtled downward through the air, crashed with devastating force upon the decks of the mighty fleet.

While Operator 5 and Tim Donovan and Captain Yarman watched breathlessly, the night became suddenly garish with the flames that sprang from ship after ship. The steady roll of the continued detonations filled the air with a noise like thunder.

What must have been in the hearts and in the minds of those aviators as they released their powerful bombs upon the enemy below? They were paying back now for the death of their comrades in the previous fight. They were paying back for the millions of Americans tortured and killed in the previous months. They were paying back for the ruined cities throughout the length and breadth of America. They were paying back with a fierce, vengeful hate, born of the misery of their friends and relatives throughout the occupied territory.

And if they had no mercy that night, if they bombed until the last enemy ship had become a crippled, sinking hulk, who can blame them?

Four hundred planes, each carrying a load of six bombs, had flown out from Richardson Bay

Now, four hundred planes with empty bomb racks turned back from the Battle of the Farallon Islands.

For five hours the *Mongol,* which was the only ship afloat, cruised over a wide radius, picking up survivors from the destroyed fleet. Then the small crew, weary and aching in every bone, turned their faces homeward.

Lester had flown his flotilla back to San Francisco Bay. In the cabin of the *Mongol,* Jimmy Christopher sat limply in a chair. The strain of the last few days had been terrific. Now the reaction was beginning to tell on him. He looked across at Captain Yarman who sat facing him, and the two men smiled.

They had engaged in an unbelievably mad undertaking, and that undertaking had been crowned with unqualified success.

"I think," Captain Yarman said slowly, "that when the Board of Governors learns of this victory, they will revoke their surrender."

Jimmy Christopher was about to reply, when Tim Donovan came lurching into the cabin. The boy's eyes were wide with excitement and consternation. His hands were trembling.

"Jimmy! I've been listening in on the air. The Central Empire troops under Marshal Kremer have smashed through our defenses in the Santa Rosa Mountains. They've thrown eighty divisions into that sector, and they're marching on San Bernardino, carrying everything before them. And the Board of Governors ordered the American Defense Forces to evacuate the Continental Divide. The Purple Armies are marching across all the passes into Wyoming and Colorado. They're cutting down to effect a junction with their other armies coming down through Southern California. It looks — as if we're licked!"

Up to that moment Operator 5 had been limp, weary, exhausted. In victory, he had become tired. Now, faced with this sudden announcement of disaster, his eyes began to sparkle, and new vitality seemed to radiate from him.

He arose quickly.

"No, Tim, we're not licked. We've just begun to fight. Captain Yarman! Order full steam ahead for San Francisco."

THE END

www.ingramcontent.com/pod-product-compliance
Lightning Source LLC
Chambersburg PA
CBHW020659180626
46816CB00003B/1358